IS STEVIE GUILTY AS CHARGED?

Carole edged Starlight closer to the scene and looked over Max's shoulder. Max shook his head as he held up the torn ends of the leather. Now everyone could see the terrible truth. The leather hadn't just ripped. It had been deliberately severed.

Carole let out an audible gasp. Someone had tried to sabotage Veronica!

"Of all the dirty tricks to pull!" Max exclaimed, looking stunned at first, and then very angry. When he uttered his next words, his voice was hard and icy. "I would like to know who, in my stable, could have done a thing like this."

At that instant, all the members of Horse Wise looked right at one person: Stevie Lake. . . .

THE SADDLE CLUB

STABLE WITCH

BONNIE BRYANT

A SKYLARK BOOK
NEW YORK • TORONTO • LONDON • SYDNEY • AUCKLAND

RL 5, 009–012

STABLE WITCH

A Bantam Skylark Book / February 1995

Skylark Books is a registered trademark of Bantam Books,
a division of Bantam Doubleday Dell Publishing Group, Inc.
Registered in U.S. Patent and Trademark Office and elsewhere.

"The Saddle Club" is a trademark of Bonnie Bryant Hiller.
The Saddle Club design/logo, which consists of
a riding crop and a riding hat, is a
trademark of Bantam Books.

ISBN 0-553-48259-9

Published simultaneously in the United States and Canada

Bantam Books are published by Bantam Books, a division of Bantam Doubleday Dell Publishing Group, Inc. Its trademark, consisting of the words
"Bantam Books" and the portrayal of a rooster, is Registered in U.S. Patent
and Trademark Office and in other countries. Marca Registrada. Bantam
Books, 1540 Broadway, New York, New York 10036.

PRINTED IN THE UNITED STATES OF AMERICA

OPM   0 9 8 7 6 5 4 3 2 1

*I would like to express my special thanks
to Caitlin C. Macy
for her help in the writing of this book.*

"SHH!" A GIGGLING Stevie Lake put her finger to her lips.

"But—" Her twin brother Alex started to protest.

Stevie motioned wildly to silence him. Alex had caught her tiptoeing downstairs in her nightgown. Of course he had immediately known that something was up. Usually Stevie leapt from her bed and galloped downstairs like a Thoroughbred in the Kentucky Derby. Today she was as quiet as a mouse. And for good reason.

Stevie's two best friends, Carole Hanson and Lisa Atwood, were sleeping over at her house. So far she had managed to get out of bed and sneak past them without waking them up. Now, all she had to do was make it downstairs and prepare "breakfast"—or at least what they would think was breakfast—to put the final twist on a perfect practical joke.

"What's going on?" Alex whispered.

Stevie shook her head and beckoned for Alex to follow her.

"All right, what are you plotting?" Alex demanded as soon as they were out of earshot in the safety of the kitchen.

Stevie smiled smugly. "Oh, just a little Saddle Club joking around," she replied. She turned her back and began to rummage in the cupboards, getting out plates, forks, knives, and napkins.

"With all the joking around *you* do, I'm surprised you're still a member of The Saddle Club," Alex muttered.

"Fortunately, being serious all the time is not a requirement for joining," Stevie retorted.

If it had been, Stevie thought, she would have long ago been kicked out of the club that she, Lisa, and Carole had started. She was constantly getting into trouble with all the jokes she played, and she was just as constantly devising clever ways of getting right back out of trouble.

There *were* two things that members of The Saddle

Club did have to be serious about: being horse-crazy and being willing to help each other out in any kind of situation. Other than those two rules, the individual members could be—and were—very different from one another. Clattering around in the kitchen, Stevie mused about just how different.

Take Carole and Lisa, for instance, asleep upstairs. Carole was probably dreaming about riding her horse, Starlight, in the Olympics. Totally dedicated to riding and all aspects of horse care, Carole wanted to grow up to be a trainer, vet, professional rider, or any one of a dozen things that meant spending one's life in a stable. Thinking about horses took up almost her every waking moment. And maybe, Stevie ventured to guess, her every sleeping moment, too.

Lisa, on the other hand, was probably not dreaming at all. She was so practical and sensible that, if anyone had asked, she would probably have said that it was silly to waste time dreaming when you could be getting a good night's rest. She swore by her early bedtime and kept to a tidy schedule of riding, homework, and chores. Sometimes she could be too strict with herself. Being in The Saddle Club had helped her to become more flexible, and she was more than willing to rearrange her plans for an adventure.

And as for herself, Stevie thought, she had hardly

been able to sleep at all, she had been so busy planning the joke she was going to play.

"So, what's the big deal?" Alex asked, startling Stevie back to attention. "It looks like you're setting the table."

Stevie gave him a withering glance. "I *am* setting the table, brother dear. And besides that, I've already made breakfast for everyone." With that, she whisked two cloth napkins off the centerpiece. Piled high on a serving platter were mounds of pancakes just begging to be eaten.

"Boy, you really outdid yourself, Stevie. These look good enough to eat . . . ," Alex began.

Stevie nodded graciously at her brother's praise.

"It's too bad they're not edible," he finished, flashing her a wicked look of triumph.

Stevie knew defeat when she heard it, especially from one of her own brothers. "How did you know?" she asked.

"Simple. We're doing the same project in my art class," Alex explained. "It's amazing how real plaster of paris can look." Eagerly he started telling her about all the things he and his friends had been making with plaster of paris during the past week, too.

"One guy did fake money—stacks of hundred-dollar

4

bills. They looked completely real. And then there was this disgusting mass of blood and guts."

"Yeah, people in my class did all that, too, but I thought fake breakfast was pretty original," Stevie put in. She explained how she had chosen to make pancakes and had paid attention to every detail—coloring the plaster a creamy white, pouring out the cakes, trimming them with a single razor blade when they were dry, and then painting the results a toasty brown.

"That's the problem with them. They look *too* good to eat. When Mom makes them, they're always all different sizes and sort of plain brown," Alex pointed out.

Stevie shrugged off the criticism. She was pretty sure Carole and Lisa would fall for it. After all, they went to the local public school—and not to Fenton Hall, the private school which Stevie and Alex attended. There was a chance their art teacher had never even heard of plaster of paris.

Before he could get away, Stevie enlisted Alex in helping her finish setting the table and getting everything all ready for Carole and Lisa, who would be coming down any minute.

The girls had planned to get up early so they could go to their Pony Club meeting together. Carole, Lisa, and Stevie all rode in Horse Wise Pony Club, which had most of its meetings at Pine Hollow Stables. It was very convenient for The Saddle Club because Pine Hollow was where they normally rode and where Stevie and Carole boarded their horses. Having Pony Club at Pine Hollow was like having a security blanket along for the ride. They knew the barn and all of the horses from top to bottom. They also knew the head instructor of both Horse Wise and Pine Hollow, Max Regnery. Max not only gave lessons there but also owned the entire farm. It had been in his family for generations.

Sure enough, Carole and Lisa appeared in the kitchen in a matter of minutes, rubbing their eyes and yawning. Alex barely looked up from shoveling cereal into his mouth when they entered. In response to Lisa and Carole's greeting, he nodded briefly.

"Boy, am I starved," Carole commented, with an appreciative glance at the breakfast table.

"Me, too," Lisa added. "I always love a good breakfast before riding."

"Good. I'm glad you guys are hungry because this should be a great meal," Stevie predicted. "Now here you go, Lisa, sit right here, and you're over here, Carole," she instructed them in her best motherly voice. First she poured some orange juice for each of them.

Then she took the plate of pancakes and began to serve them.

"Wow, you made pancakes—yum!" Carole exclaimed.

"Yes, I do aim to please," Stevie said. She took a furtive glance at Lisa, who was eyeing her plate suspiciously. "Here, they need butter," Stevie said, smearing some all over Lisa's plate for her.

"Uh, thanks," Lisa said, taken aback at Stevie's zealous hostessing.

"And, ah, don't forget to sweeten them up," Stevie said. She reached for the jug of syrup and began drowning Lisa's pancakes in the gooey liquid.

Lisa picked up her fork. She paused. She looked at Carole, who was now pouring syrup over her plate. She looked at Stevie, who was now chowing down a bowl of cereal. She put her fork down.

"Yikes!" Carole, who had been struggling to cut her pancakes, let out a shriek of horror as her knife bent in two.

Lisa folded her arms across her chest. "All right, Stevie, where'd you get the plaster of paris?" she asked grimly.

Stevie smiled wanly. "I—well—I—" Abruptly she snapped her mouth shut and glanced at Alex for help.

7

"Oh, no. No *way* are you going to drag me into this one, Stevie," Alex declared.

"Very funny, Stevie," Carole commented wryly. "Fake pancakes—ha, ha, ha."

"Yeah—hysterical," Lisa added sarcastically.

But Stevie was grinning from ear to ear. "That was so f-funny!" She managed between peals of laughter. "You guys r-r-really thought I made p-pan-pancakes!"

Lisa and Carole exchanged glances, sighing audibly. They were used to Stevie's finding her own jokes infinitely more funny than they did. They knew the best thing to do was to sit calmly and wait until Stevie had gotten control over herself once again.

Still snorting with laughter, Stevie remembered her hostessing duties, this time for real. She got up and took out bowls and a box of cereal from the pantry. "I wanted to do fake cereal and put it in the real boxes, but I figured it would take too long to color the individual flakes and raisins."

"Boy, it's really a shame that you didn't have time," Lisa remarked flatly.

After pouring them bowls of cereal, Stevie excused herself to go hunt for her breeches in the laundry room. At the Lakes' house Stevie and her brothers shared the chores. In the past, that had made for some interestingly colored wash loads. So now Stevie always washed her riding clothes herself. It was a pretty good system, except for the fact that she never remembered her dirty breeches until the morning of Pony Club.

Today, even the thought of having to do a last-minute spot cleaning didn't seem to bother her, though. Lisa and Carole could hear her guffawing all the way down the hall. As soon as she was out of earshot, they started giggling, too. They couldn't decide which was funnier—Stevie's dumb joke or Stevie's *reaction* to her dumb joke.

"Well," said Lisa, between bites, "this is about what you'd expect."

"What is?" Carole asked curiously.

"This morning. It's about what you'd expect for the typical beginning of a day with The Saddle Club."

At the sound of Stevie's howls drifting through the house, Carole had to agree.

THE REST OF the morning followed a typical Saddle
Club routine as well. The girls got dressed in their
medium-good riding clothes, walked over to Pine
Hollow, groomed and tacked up their horses, and met
in the indoor ring for a mounted meeting.

Carole was riding her own horse, Starlight, a bay
Thoroughbred gelding, named for the eye-catching
white star in the middle of his forehead. The two
made a pretty picture: Carole's jet-black hair and dark
eyes matched Starlight's mane and tail.

Stevie was aboard Belle. She could still hardly believe that the dark bay, half-Arabian, half-Saddlebred
mare was hers to keep. Shortly after Stevie's parents

had bought the horse, they had discovered that Belle was stolen property. Eventually things had gotten straightened out with Belle's legal owner, and now the mare truly belonged to Stevie. After weeks of deliberations about what to name her, Stevie had recently christened her Belle because of her American Saddlebred breeding and because she was feisty and independent, a lot like a famous Southern belle—Scarlett O'Hara. A lot of the riders at Pine Hollow thought Belle was a lot like Stevie, too—feisty and spirited. Stevie herself absolutely agreed—those traits were part of what she loved about the horse.

By pure coincidence, Lisa's mount was a bay, too. Lisa didn't own the mare, but Max let her be Prancer's usual rider. She loved learning together with Prancer and found the young, inexperienced horse both challenging and very rewarding to ride.

Today as Lisa looked around at the rest of the Horse Wise riders, she realized that she was unusually nervous about keeping up in the lesson. So far, everything had gone fine. They had all warmed up and trotted over low fences to get ready to jump while Max had set up a course of eight jumps.

Normally, Lisa didn't worry about her ability. Even though she had started riding later than Carole and Stevie, she had learned fast and was constantly improving. But today's class was going to focus on jump-ing, an area where Lisa felt less secure. She gulped a bit as she looked over the course. Unlike her old mount, Barq, who was a seasoned school horse, Prancer was relatively new to jumping. She tended to look twice at anything funny-looking, and she often overjumped by a couple of feet, jarring Lisa's position in the saddle.

"Boy, I hope Belle behaves herself," Stevie, who had elected to ride first, murmured as she rode by Lisa. Lisa gave her an encouraging smile. It helped to hear that not everyone knew for sure that they would do the course perfectly. After all, Lisa told herself, Belle was still new to Pine Hollow. Stevie hadn't jumped her much yet, and there was no telling how they'd do.

Stevie was the first rider to take a turn. She picked up a rhythmic canter and started for the first fence. Belle cleared it easily and, prepared by Stevie in mid-air, turned immediately for the second jump when they landed.

Lisa's heart sank as she saw how confident Stevie looked. A split second later, guilt washed over her. How could she have been hoping that Stevie would have problems with Belle?

It's just that I don't want to be the only rider to need help from Max, Lisa told herself. Stevie and Carole could get a donkey over the course if they had to. Even if their mount wasn't perfect, they were always in control. Lisa, on the other hand, relied more on her horse to carry her than on her own ability to make the horse behave well.

Stevie finished the course and pulled up smartly. She turned to the onlookers and asked innocently, "I guess she's a real jumper, huh?" Stevie was glowing with pleasure at Belle's success. Except for Veronica diAngelo, the rest of Horse Wise looked almost as pleased as Stevie. The Pony Club often traveled to compete in regional rallies where the combined score of the team was what mattered. So it was always good news when a good jumper joined the team.

"I guess she's a real *packer*," Veronica said, loud enough for Stevie to hear.

Stevie didn't even bother to retort. "Packer" was slang for a horse who "packed" his or her rider over every fence, without the rider's having to do anything. Stevie knew that riding her skittish half-Arab was no easy task, and she wasn't going to waste her breath debating Veronica—at least not right this second when Carole was starting her round.

Starlight was truly in his element over fences. He had wonderful form and happily pricked up his ears at every fence. Carole's only problem was keeping him slow and steady enough to make all of the turns. It took her a full circle after the course to get him to slow to a trot. Still, Max seemed pleased with their ride. Like everyone else, he liked watching the beautiful horse do what he did best—and Carole's skill only enhanced the picture.

Lisa felt a little better when she saw Veronica do the course on Garnet. Every time they went over a jump, the girl ducked down toward Garnet's shoulder and shoved her hands way up around Garnet's ears. Max had to speak to her a number of times.

First he told her she was exaggerating her form. "You're jumping less than three feet, Veronica. Don't make it look like you're going over a six-foot wall!"

"It's not my fault these jumps are so tiny!" Veronica wailed, snatching at the bit in frustration.

"Don't you dare take it out on your horse!" Max warned. Above all other things, The Saddle Club knew, Max despised it when a rider punished her horse for her own problems. "And prepare for the jumps much earlier!" he added. Too late, Veronica careened toward the final obstacle. She was going so fast that Garnet missed the jump altogether and cantered right by it. Max made her slow to a trot and take the last fence by itself. Never one to withhold criti-

14

cism where it was due, he called cheerfully after her, "Lots of work to do, Veronica! Lots and lots!"

Veronica clenched her teeth and jumped off Garnet. "I've had just about enough for today," she muttered. Then, seeing Lisa shorten her reins and prepare to trot off, she added, "At least I'm not on some crazy horse from the track who probably doesn't even know what a jump is."

Lisa cringed at Veronica's words even though she knew they weren't true. Prancer was no more crazy than Garnet. Her coming from the racetrack just meant she had been trained differently. And Lisa had already jumped her a few times before, so the mare obviously knew how. But then why did Lisa have a sick feeling in the pit of her stomach at the sight of all of those jumps?

Grimly, she gritted her teeth and headed for the first one, an inviting picket fence. The white slats shone brightly in front of her. They looked almost like teeth, ready to bite . . .

Right before the takeoff, Lisa dropped her hands and fell forward on Prancer's neck. The mare managed to clear the fence, but she felt unsteady. Prancer got over the next jump, too, and the ones after that. But instead of relaxing, Lisa felt herself tense up on every approach. She felt half frozen in the saddle, and

15

she couldn't make herself concentrate. She knew she wasn't helping Prancer at all. When she finished, Max told her that she was having a little trouble, but nothing he didn't think she could cure.

Rejoining the others, Lisa felt frustrated and envious. She wanted Prancer to be as good as Starlight and Belle, and she wanted to be as good as Carole and Stevie and the others. It didn't help that she had already missed two chances to do well with Prancer. Several months ago she had competed in a horse show with Prancer before she or the horse was ready. The day had ended in the embarrassment of being disqualified. Then she had planned to compete in a Pony Club dressage rally but had been forced to quit when the starring role in a local production of *Annie* had left her with insufficient practice time. Now she was eager for some real success on the horse. She didn't want to have to content herself with just "getting around" the course—she wanted to put in a really great round. Being a practical thinker, she realized that the only thing she could do now was to decide to work very hard on jumping. Silently, she promised herself that she would follow through on her decision.

AFTER CLASS HORSE Wise met in the tack room for a talk while they cleaned their bridles and saddles. Calling the meeting to order, Max complimented them on their jumping. Then he paused to survey the group of riders before him.

"You might as well get it over with and make the big announcement," Stevie teased. She knew Max well enough to recognize that when he had something special to say, he always got a twinkle in his eye and tried to build up the suspense.

In spite of himself, Max burst out laughing. "All right, all right. So much for surprises. Here's what gives: I've always wanted to open up Pine Hollow to the local riding community and hold a schooling show here. So, guess what? I've decided that two weekends from now is the perfect time for the First Annual Pine Hollow Invitational Schooling Show. Does that qualify as a big announcement, Stevie?"

Stevie nodded vigorously. She, Lisa, and Carole glanced at one another with excitement. A schooling show was like the best of both worlds. You got to compete for real, with real judges and real horse show classes, but you didn't have to go through all the efforts of getting ready for real. You didn't have to give baths, braid, and polish tack till four in the morning, and, with the show at Pine Hollow, they wouldn't even have to get up early to trailer over.

When the chatter had died down, Max explained

he was going to be inviting a few other Pony Clubs to send riders although all of the competition would be individual. The show would consist entirely of jumping classes in three divisions—hunters, jumpers, and equitation. "Can anyone explain the difference?" Max asked.

Carole's hand shot up. She dreamed about riding in horse shows so often, she could have recited the difference in her sleep. "In jumper classes, they judge how fast and clean you jump. In hunter classes, they judge the horse's form. And in equitation, they judge the rider's form."

"Precisely," Max said. He raised his eyebrows. "Now, can anyone guess which classes I want all of you to ride in?"

"Hmm . . . let's see . . . equitation?" Lisa said, pretending to mull over the choices. She knew as well as anyone that Max was more of a stickler for good equitation than any other aspect of riding.

"Right again. You're all going in Junior Equitation Over Fences."

"But—" Stevie began.

"End of discussion," Max announced. "Except for one last thing. As I have in the past, I'd like you all to write down your goals for the show." As he handed out pieces of paper, Max reminded each of them that her most important competitor was herself. "Work on being the best rider you can be. Don't worry about beating anyone else." With that, he turned and was out the door.

Stevie sighed. She had been about to explain that she thought it was really much more important for Belle to get an opportunity to show what a great jumper she was than for her to show what a great equitator—if that was a word—she was.

With pencil in hand, she gazed around the room. As she stared at the bent head of Veronica diAngelo, Stevie could feel her jaw set in a determined line. There was no way on earth she was going to let Miss-Snotty-Nose beat her, especially not after her comment today.

Stevie glanced back at the paper. She couldn't exactly say that beating Veronica was her one and only goal. It would be very bad sportsmanship—not to mention the fact that Max would find it unacceptable.

"My goal for the schooling show is to improve my position over fences," she wrote finally. There. That would meet Max's requirements *and* it was the truth. If she had to take posture lessons every day and walk with books on her head for two weeks straight, she was going to beat Veronica in equitation.

Next to Stevie, Carole chewed on her pencil. She

had written, "*My goal is for Starlight and me to enjoy ourselves, and for Starlight to get more exposure to competition, and for me to be able to keep him quiet in the ring and not let him speed up at the end of the course.*" She hoped it wasn't too wordy, but she really had a lot to say. She could hardly wait until the show. It would be an incredible treat for both her and Starlight to ride only in jumping classes.

Lisa was still contemplating her piece of paper. As she pondered, she glimpsed Veronica out of the corner of her eye, shoving her paper into her pocket. "Aren't you going to write anything?" Lisa asked.

"No, I'm not, as a matter of fact. I'm going to give Max a blank piece of paper if you must know," Veronica retorted. "Because I'm going to *blank out* all the other riders! Get it? I'm going to win, no matter what it takes." With that, she gave the group an icy stare and strode off.

"That's what you think," Stevie muttered darkly.

Lisa just shook her head. Veronica's response was exactly what she expected. She glanced back down at the paper. It certainly was tempting to focus on winning. After all, who wouldn't kill for a blue ribbon in equitation? Sure, it was only a schooling show, but with the personalities at Pine Hollow, it might end up being more competitive than a real show.

Lisa wasn't about to make the same mistake—not being prepared—as she had at the other show where Prancer had been disqualified. Frowning over the piece of paper, she slowly wrote, *"I am going to work very hard for the next two weeks and at the show to jump more confidently so that Prancer will, too. I am going to do the best I can to get her ready for the show and to ride well on the day of the show."* And, Lisa added silently to herself, I'm going to start right now.

"Coming, Lisa?" Stevie asked. She and Carole had put their tack away and were making plans to go back to the Lakes' and hang out for the afternoon.

"No, I don't think so. I've got some work to do here," Lisa answered. There, she had done it. By deciding to stay at Pine Hollow, she had already started to work toward her goal.

WHEN CAROLE AND Stevie had left, Lisa returned to Prancer's stall. She had decided to check over her grooming job. As Max always said, grooming was an important part of success in any riding competition— horsemanship began from the ground up.

Thinking of the ground prompted Lisa to look at Prancer's hooves. She seemed to remember skimping a little on picking them out after the lesson. She cross tied Prancer and methodically picked up her feet, one by one. Sure enough, the near hind hoof betrayed her sloppiness: there was a small flat stone lodged between the shoe and heel. Chastising herself for her careless-ness, Lisa began to dig it out gently.

It took a while to remove. Finally she stood up, satisfied but sorry that Prancer had had to suffer even a minor discomfort. She then began to go over the mare's coat, mane, and tail until they gleamed. Already, Lisa felt better about the morning's practice. She had no idea why she had felt so insecure, but she knew that she could ride well at the show if she prepared extra hard. She planned to work on every last detail of her position, from head to toe. There was no reason why she and Prancer couldn't be as good as the others. They would just have to put in more hours, since they had the handicap of their own inexperience.

"There," Lisa said, stepping back to survey her grooming job. "You look clean enough to eat off of."

"Wish I could say the same about my kitchen floor," Mrs. Reg commented, joining Lisa in the aisle. "But I'm afraid it's covered with riding boots, bran mash, and horsehair as usual."

Lisa laughed and greeted Mrs. Reg warmly. Max's mother was a favorite among The Saddle Club. She always seemed to be around to lend a helping hand or a sympathetic ear. She knew more about horses than almost anyone, but she never made a rider feel stupid or ignorant. "Still grooming, huh?" Mrs. Reg asked.

Lisa nodded. "With two weeks to the schooling

show, I've got a lot of work to do. I figured I'd start today with doing a better job of grooming."

"Good idea," Mrs. Reg said approvingly. "It should be a great day. We're expecting about thirty Pine Hollow students and thirty outsiders, so that will keep it manageable. And the judges are all well known to Max and me."

"That's good to hear," Lisa said. She knew how important it was to find judges you could trust. Horse shows were incredibly subjective. At their level, there wasn't usually too much question over the placement. But at top-level shows, like the American Horse Show, the horses and riders were so evenly matched that it was nearly impossible to understand how the judges could differentiate.

In addition to knowing lots about horses, Mrs. Reg had a knack for getting at whatever was bothering any of the Pine Hollow students, no matter how hard they tried to pretend that everything was fine. Today was no different. She watched Lisa rubbing Prancer for a few minutes and then asked, "So, are you looking forward to jumping? Max told me he's entered your whole lesson group in Equitation Over Fences."

Lisa sighed. There was no point in trying to keep a stiff upper lip around Mrs. Reg. Besides, it might make her feel better to admit her insecurity. She looked up at the older woman, a timid expression on her face. "To be honest, Mrs. Reg," she admitted, "I'm not so sure. I mean, I love jumping, and I love Prancer, but jumping Prancer—I don't know. It's definitely going to be a challenge. Today we had some problems. I was convinced the jumps were going to attack me!"

Mrs. Reg nodded sympathetically. "Everyone probably feels that way at one time or another," she said, "even Nigel Hawthorne."

Lisa smiled. Nigel Hawthorne was a member of the British Equestrian Team and the husband of Dorothy DeSoto, a former Pine Hollow rider. Nigel regularly jumped six-foot fences and higher. It was hard to imagine him thinking a picket rail had teeth! "In any case," Lisa said, forcing herself to sound confident, "I'm going to put in extra hours this week and next to make sure we're ready—if that's all right with you and Max."

"That's fine, Lisa. Will Stevie and Carole be joining you?" Mrs. Reg asked. Max's mother was fully aware of the three girls' tight friendship.

Lisa shook her head. "I don't think so. You should have seen Belle and Starlight today—they definitely don't need the extra practice."

Mrs. Reg frowned ever so slightly. "Does that mean you want to beat your friends?" she inquired.

"Oh, *no*, Mrs. Reg!" Lisa cried. It had never even occurred to her that she would do better than Carole and Stevie. She tried to explain. "I'm not trying to beat them—I just want to do well myself, and they're the standard that I measure myself against."

Mrs. Reg looked pleased with Lisa's response. "So you'll be coming to Pine Hollow more often for the next couple of weeks?"

Lisa explained that she was hoping to come in the mornings—starting with tomorrow morning. Mrs. Reg agreed to let her ride at seven A.M. the next day. "You know, this reminds me of a young man who . . ."

Lisa bit her lip. Mrs. Reg had a habit of launching into lengthy, seemingly pointless stories when she wanted to tell a rider something. Lisa knew another story was coming.

"Anyway," Mrs. Reg went on, oblivious to Lisa's reaction, "this young man used to ride at Pine Hollow, and he competed in lots of three-day events."

Lisa tried to listen attentively. The story was about a rider whose horse was just fine in the ring at jumping and dressage but had a lot of trouble in practice with the cross-country course. First the horse and rider would be off the pace—too slow—and come in over the allowed time, which meant receiving time penalties. Another time, the rider would forget the course and miss a couple of fences or do them out of order. And once he had just plain gotten lost on the course.

"The funny thing was," Mrs. Reg continued, her eyes staring off into space, "every time he went out on the cross-country course, he thought he saw the same girl. On his very first ride, he thought this girl had intentionally spooked his horse at one of the fences. The next time he went out, he caught a glimpse of her midway through the course. It took him five or six tries to get his horse over it, and it made him so furious and upset he couldn't finish the course.

"After that, she was everywhere. He saw her at the starting gate; he saw her on the trail; he saw her lurking near fences. He even thought he saw her reflection at the water jump. First he thought perhaps she was just a spectator who happened to turn up to watch him practice. Then he thought maybe it was another competitor from Pine Hollow who wanted to see how he was doing. He got more and more flustered, and every time he went out on a course, he did poorly."

Lisa shook her head. The poor guy, she thought.

"He asked everybody around the stable if they had ever seen her," Mrs. Reg continued. "But none of them knew who he was talking about." The older woman paused dramatically.

"So?" Lisa demanded, her brow furrowed into confusion at what Mrs. Reg was trying to get at.

Mrs. Reg looked gravely at Lisa. Her voice grew quiet. "So? So, he came to think of her as a witch who had cast a spell on him and his horse."

Lisa snorted with laughter. "But Mrs. Reg," Lisa began, trying to recover her composure. After all, she didn't want to be downright rude. "Everyone knows there's no such thing as witches."

Mrs. Reg shrugged. "Let's just say I'm not so sure about that."

"What do you mean?" Lisa demanded. She was beginning to feel frustrated by the whole cryptic story.

"Do I really have to explain the whole thing?" Mrs. Reg asked. She sounded a little annoyed that Lisa hadn't gotten the point yet. "All right, I'll tell you how the story ends, and then you'll see what I'm getting at. At the three-day event, the boy did very well in dressage and jumped clean in stadium. But he racked up so many points in cross-country that he didn't even get a ribbon for his overall performance. Once again, he had seen the girl. And until the day he moved away from Pine Hollow, he always swore that there was a witch at the stable who had put a hex on him. He never did do our cross-country course clean."

"So, was the boy right or wrong—about the witch?" Lisa asked, hoping for an explanation even though she didn't believe in witches.

Mrs. Reg glanced at her watch. "Oh, dear me, the time. And I was supposed to have these show schedules printed up at the copy shop for Max already. Well, I'd better run—can't stand around all day telling old stories . . ." Before Lisa could get another word in, Mrs. Reg had bustled down the aisle.

Lisa had to laugh. Obviously Mrs. Reg was implying something that she wanted Lisa to understand—but what? Lisa tried to figure out the meaning on her own, but it was useless. Was Mrs. Reg trying to tell her that, even though Halloween had been months ago, Pine Hollow was haunted by its very own stable witch? If that was true—which, of course, rational Lisa knew wasn't—then what was she supposed to do about it? The very thought made her giggle. Imagine going to Stevie and Carole and telling them that their next Saddle Club project was going to be doing some serious witch-hunting at Pine Hollow. They would think she was off her rocker.

"But we'll keep our eyes open for brooms that fly, won't we, Prancer?" Lisa whispered to the mare. She gave her a quick hug, promising to be back at seven the next morning to work on jumping. "We're going to improve so fast, nobody will recognize us, right?"

Lisa had to take Prancer's methodical hay chewing as a "yes."

THE NEXT MORNING Lisa fairly leapt out of bed. She had spent the evening writing down a few more things she had thought of to work on. Her new list was sort of an expansion of what she had put down as her goal for the schooling show. When the alarm rang at five after six, she could hardly wait to get over to Pine Hollow and put her intentions into practice.

It was exciting being at the stable so early—6:45, to be exact. It felt as if she were going to a horse show and had come to braid or put a final shine on her tack. Even Prancer seemed to sense the specialness of the occasion. When Lisa led her out to the cross ties to groom her, she swiveled her ears back and forth, all attention. Lisa went about her brushing happily, whistling and chatting to Prancer. Yesterday's bad lesson seemed ages ago.

Just as she was thinking how nice and peaceful Pine Hollow was in the early morning, Lisa heard a loud screech of brakes outside in the driveway. Prancer jumped, startled by the noise. "Maybe somebody else had the same idea we did," Lisa muttered, wondering who else would want to show up so early.

She had to stop her jaw from dropping when she heard, coming from the driveway, the unmistakable voice of Veronica diAngelo.

"Be back in an hour to pick me up. And don't be late, Mother," the voice warned snappily. Sure enough, a few seconds later, Veronica strode through the barn doors, tapping her English jumping bat against her custom-made boots.

Veronica had the same reaction upon seeing Lisa that Lisa had had when she heard Veronica. She stopped in her tracks, and her lips turned down in a classic Veronica pout. "What are *you* doing here?" she demanded.

"I was going to ask you the same thing," Lisa replied evasively. She wasn't about to let on that she was practicing for the show—that would be like begging Veronica to make a rude remark about her jumping ability.

Veronica snorted. "Look, you can drop the act because obviously we're both here for the same reason: the schooling show, right?"

Lisa nodded cautiously. She still couldn't believe Veronica had shown up this early in the morning to put in some hard work on her riding. "Early morning" and "hard work" were not usually concepts that one used in the same sentence with "Veronica diAngelo."

"Fine. I'll see you in the indoor," Veronica said. Then she turned and stomped off to get Garnet.

Lisa stared after her. Veronica was actually going to groom and tack up her own horse? Usually, she made Red, the head stablehand, do it. This morning was already turning out to be stranger than Lisa had expected.

In a few minutes, Lisa was mounted and warming up in the ring. She half hoped that she could finish her schooling before Veronica came in, but she knew that was wishful thinking. With the girl's slapdash grooming style, no doubt she'd be ready in about thirty seconds.

There was no getting around it: Veronica's presence made Lisa both uneasy and annoyed. More accurately, she thought, she was annoyed because she was uneasy.

The whole point of the morning was for her to get in some quality practice time with Prancer—free from distractions. Now she would have to worry about how she looked in front of Veronica, instead of just concentrating on herself. "But we'll show her, won't we, Prancer?" Lisa said aloud.

The sliding door opened and Veronica led Garnet into the ring. Ignoring them, Lisa jammed her heels down and took a firmer grip on the reins. Silently she vowed not to be shaken by any obnoxious thing Veronica could think of to say.

"What are you planning on doing about a course?" Veronica asked.

Lisa paused. She had been so steeled for a critical barb that it took her a couple of seconds to realize that Veronica had actually asked an intelligent question. What was more, she, Lisa, had forgotten all about setting up the jumps because Max usually did it for them. It would be a pain to get off Prancer now and have to re–warm up after erecting a course.

"Never mind. Since you're already warming up, I'll put up some cross rails and verticals before I get on," Veronica volunteered quickly, tying Garnet. "Then I thought we could critique each other's performance."

Now Lisa really couldn't believe her ears—or eyes. She watched, incredulous, as Veronica dragged a bunch of poles and standards out and made a few fences for them to school over. Then, without another word, she got on and began her warm-up walk, trot, and canter in a businesslike manner. Evidently, Lisa realized with amazement, Veronica was as serious about practicing as she was. Just then Prancer shied at a shadow in the ring. Shaken, Lisa reminded herself to quit staring at Veronica and start concentrating on her own horse. The mare felt a bit skittish, and Lisa hoped it was just the strange hour. Prancer wasn't accustomed to being tacked up and exercised so early in the morning.

After a few minutes, Veronica waved Lisa down to her end of the ring. "What's the matter—don't you want to trot the cross rail?" she asked.

"Of course I do," Lisa snapped defensively. The truth was, as Veronica had probably guessed, she hadn't wanted to be the one to start jumping first. Of course it would make sense for her to go before Veronica, considering that she'd been warming up longer. "I just wanted to make sure Prancer was ready," she explained. The excuse sounded lame even to her.

"Well, Garnet's ready, so you can watch me go first, okay?" Without waiting for an answer, Veronica headed for the fence.

"Sure," Lisa muttered. "Go right ahead." It was one

of those situations where she couldn't win. Either she would go first and, more likely than not, mess up out of nervousness, or Veronica would go first and jump perfectly, making Lisa even more anxious about doing well herself. The Arabian approached the cross rail at a rhythmic trot. Veronica stayed balanced in the saddle, her seat lifted slightly in proper jumping position. In the air she released the reins, leaned forward, and landed neatly on the other side.

"That looked pretty good," Lisa called in a strangled voice. She had forgotten that when Veronica concentrated, she could compete with the best. This morning she was definitely concentrating. She put Garnet over the warm-up jump a number of times, making her trot it and canter it, and stopping neatly after the jump each time. Lisa stared at the two of them glumly. She just knew she couldn't match their performance. After all, Garnet was much better trained than Prancer, and much more experienced.

After her fifth or sixth near-perfect jump, Veronica told Lisa she could give it a go.

"Thanks," Lisa muttered sarcastically under her breath. "It's so nice of you to let me have a turn." She picked up the reins and asked for a trot. As soon as she turned toward the jump, she tensed up in her back and neck and arms. It felt as if her body were set in concrete, and she couldn't move out of the position.

The jump came closer and closer. Lisa stared at the white and red stripes of the crossed poles, feeling almost dizzy. A few strides before the cross rail, she dropped her hands entirely, resting them uselessly on Prancer's neck. The mare half stumbled over the low X. It was exactly the same mistake Lisa had made in the lesson.

Before Veronica could comment, Lisa called, "Let me try that again. I wasn't really—"

"Oh, I know what your problem is," Veronica announced, all enthusiasm. "Really, you shouldn't worry about it. It's typical of a lot of beginning riders. You're looking down and you're dropping her at the fence. . . ."

As Veronica droned on, Lisa simmered with rage at the word "beginning." She knew she still was a beginner in some ways, but hearing Veronica's condescending tone of voice made her want to strangle someone —the obvious choice was Veronica. A tiny part of her knew that Veronica was right, but she was so upset she couldn't listen. And she definitely couldn't concentrate on all of her mistakes at once. "I *know* I'm dropping her. That's why I want to do it again—obviously," she said.

"Well, you know it's never a good idea to just keep doing things again and again without knowing what's wrong," Veronica replied cheerily. "I just thought I'd explain one or two alterations you could make to—"

"I told you, I know what's wrong!" Lisa practically screamed. Angrily she picked up a trot again and headed toward the fence. Prancer felt unsure beneath her, surprised at the quick pace. This time, Lisa swore she wouldn't drop her hands before Prancer had jumped—and she succeeded. Or at least she succeeded in not dropping her hands. Unfortunately, she forgot to release the reins at all, and she ended up jerking Prancer in the mouth. The mare threw her head up in annoyance.

"That time you—" Veronica began.

"Don't tell me! I know! I jerked her in the mouth. Big deal—so I made a mistake. I'll do it over, okay?" Lisa could hardly believe how she sounded—just like Veronica on a bad day. She halted Prancer at the end of the ring. She didn't want Veronica to see the tears of frustration welling up in her eyes.

"Lisa," Veronica began, her voice sickly sweet, "maybe you shouldn't keep jumping if you're going to get so worked up. It's really not good for Prancer's training. You should wait until you're in a calmer state

38

of mind. A green horse can be ruined with an impatient trainer."

Lisa bit her lip as hard as she could. Veronica, who was known for hitting Garnet with her crop and jerking on the reins whenever anything went wrong, was telling her to calm down? The injustice of the situation made Lisa seethe. And the worst thing was that she herself knew that she really shouldn't be jumping when she was so upset.

"Why don't you go again, Veronica?" Lisa forced herself to say. She loosened her reins and took deep breaths and stroked Prancer's neck to try to relax. There was no point in getting angry at Veronica and then taking it out on Prancer, and she knew it.

Veronica didn't need to be asked twice to perform for an audience, even an audience of one. She immediately swung into action. She took Garnet around the other four fences twice in a row, making it look as easy as pie. Lisa knew she was still exaggerating her jumping position—acting as if the jumps were bigger than they were. Still, other than her tendency to show off, she looked good and made Garnet behave nicely.

"So, how was that?" Veronica asked when she had finished.

"Great, just great," Lisa said quietly, her eyes on the

ground. She refused to elaborate any more. It disgusted her that Veronica would be practically begging for praise when obviously she knew she had ridden well.

"Really? Aw, that's sweet of you, Lisa. Thanks loads for watching. You were a great critic. Well, I've got to run. So, tah-tah for now."

Lisa watched Veronica dismount and head in. She wasn't about to remind her that she ought to cool down Garnet before putting the mare away. Veronica would probably just make another comment about "beginning" riders or something.

At the door, Veronica turned. "Good luck with your jumping, Lisa. In another couple of years, you and Prancer could be doing just as well as Garnet and I do."

Lisa didn't even bother to reply. She jumped off Prancer with one thought in her mind: letting herself have a good cry. She buried her face in Prancer's neck. Then she stopped herself. Crying wasn't going to solve anything, and it wasn't even going to make her feel better. The only thing that would make her feel better was *getting* better. And the only way to get better—and stop being bothered by Veronica—was through hard work. She had made it here at 6:45 once, and she would come again.

She looked over at the cross rail that had tripped her up. The sight of it actually brought a smile to her lips. It couldn't have been more than eighteen inches high. To prove something to herself, Lisa led Prancer over to the jump and jumped over it on foot. "If I can do it by myself, I can do it on a fifteen-plus-hand horse," she said aloud.

In a flash of determination, she got back on Prancer. She took a deep breath, asked for a trot, and headed toward the little jump.

This time, Prancer trotted over it as if it were nothing. Lisa cried out jubilantly. Then she leaned over and patted Prancer's neck gratefully. "We did it!" she whispered. "A perfect jump."

LISA REMINDED HERSELF of the perfect jump when she got dropped off at Pine Hollow for her usual riding class on Tuesday afternoon. She knew every jump could be like that if she tried hard—she just knew it.

Stevie and Carole had beaten her to Pine Hollow and were changing in the locker room when she came in. Not surprisingly, the topic of discussion was the schooling show. Carole was saying that she had dug out a couple of old books on equitation from her vast library of horse books and had been reading them in the evenings.

Joining them at her locker, Lisa commented drily,

"Of course you don't even touch the horse books until every single bit of your homework is finished."

"Oh, of *course* not," Carole replied, not missing a beat. "It wouldn't even cross my mind. You know how much more I care about math word problems than jumping positions."

"Same here," Stevie chimed in. "My mother practically has to drag me away from my homework and force me to come over to Pine Hollow when it's time for our lesson."

After the three girls had stopped giggling, Lisa asked Carole and Stevie whether they'd heard the news about Horse Wise on Saturday.

"What news?" Carole inquired. "As far as I know it's a regular Pony Club meeting."

"Not exactly. It turns out that the judges for the schooling show are going to be there watching," Lisa said.

"You're kidding—really? Isn't that illegal or something?" Stevie asked.

Lisa shrugged. "Normally, it would be kind of questionable, but since it's only a schooling show, it doesn't matter. They can even give us advice and help us out with problems. And it gives them a chance to get to know the lay of the land at Pine Hollow," Lisa explained.

"I think that's great. We'll have two chances to ride well for them, instead of one," Carole said optimistically. After Saturday's Horse Wise, she was even more excited about having the judges see Starlight. She felt like a proud mother who couldn't wait to show off how smart her baby was.

"So, how did you find out the judges were coming?" Stevie asked.

Lisa quickly filled her friends in on her early-morning jumping practice on Sunday. She had run into Max on her way out that morning. He had mentioned the judges and told her to spread the word.

Carole and Stevie both looked up from yanking on their breeches.

"Why didn't you tell us that you were coming early to practice?" Stevie asked.

"Yeah, we could have come and practiced, too—or helped you," Carole said.

Suddenly, Lisa realized how her revelation must sound to her friends—as if she were hiding something from them. The truth was she had wanted to come alone so she could clear her head completely from Saturday's lesson. And she had wanted to be able to think about her goals on her own, without any interruptions, even good ones, from The Saddle Club. Lisa struggled to put her thoughts into words. "I wasn't trying to be secretive about it," she said. "But I did like the idea of working on my own for a while. And besides, you guys don't need the practice, remember?"

Carole was completely sympathetic. "Sometimes it is better to work with just your horse and no one else around. I love schooling Starlight by myself."

"That was my plan, anyway," Lisa continued. "It turned out to be mostly a waste of time because about fifteen minutes after I got here, who shows up but Veronica."

"Veronica?" Carole and Stevie demanded in unison. They couldn't have looked more surprised if Lisa had told them she had gotten straight F's on her report card.

Lisa nodded. "Believe it or not, Veronica diAngelo was putting in extra practice time at seven in the morning."

"Are you sure you weren't seeing things, Lisa?" Carole asked anxiously.

"Yeah. Or maybe you were dreaming," Stevie ventured.

"My eyesight's fine, thank you very much, and seeing Veronica was more like a nightmare than a dream," Lisa countered. In order to prove that the morning had really happened, she told them about how much Veronica had been showing off. "She was so condescending that almost the whole practice was torture. Basically she told me that if I worked hard for about a hundred years I might be good enough to kiss her feet."

The girls laughed.

"Veronica probably dreams about opportunities like that—being alone at the stable with someone she thinks wants her advice," Carole said.

"I'm just mad that I let her get to me. It was supposed to be a morning of confidence-building," said Lisa.

"I still don't see why you didn't mention it," Stevie commented. She sounded somewhat miffed. "As a matter of fact, Carole and I can always use the practice—or at least I can. Especially with a new horse."

Lisa knew in an instant what the slight irritation in Stevie's voice meant: her naturally competitive instincts were coming out. She hated the thought of someone's preparing harder for the show than she was.

Lisa decided to get right to the point. "Listen, Stevie, you know as well as I that a few extra hours of jumping is never going to make Prancer and me good enough to beat you and Belle. It's not like you have anything to fear from me, competition-wise."

Stevie looked surprised by Lisa's comment. She paused before answering her. Finally she said,

"Thanks, Lisa, but to be honest, it's not you I'm worried about." In a nice way, Stevie explained that she knew that she was better than Lisa, just the same way she knew that Carole was better than she was. But she lived in fear at the thought of losing to Veronica. "Or not exactly fear—more like vile disgust. I just hate the idea that somebody as terrible as Veronica could be better at something than I am. I mean, she's so bad, how could she ever be good?"

At Stevie's unusual phrasing, Carole and Lisa cracked up. They didn't like to see Veronica win, either. But somehow they didn't take her failures and successes quite as personally as Stevie. If Stevie, instead of Lisa, had run into Veronica on Sunday, she probably would have set up a course of six-foot fences and dared Veronica to jump them.

"Seriously, what do you think her chances are to beat me?" Stevie asked. In her own mind, she set the odds at about 50-50. When Veronica focused, there was no telling how well she would ride. She was a "prettier" rider than Stevie was, but she was also likely to lose her temper if one little thing went wrong. Part of the question was whether, in the judges' minds, Stevie's "get-the-job-done" style would compare with Veronica's picture-perfect posing.

Before Lisa or Carole could answer, the locker room

door swung open, and Veronica herself walked in. The Saddle Club immediately stopped talking and busied themselves with changing as fast as they could.

HALF AN HOUR later the group was mounted and warming up in the outdoor ring. To their surprise, class that day was to be entirely on the flat instead of over fences. Everyone seemed relieved when Max made the announcement—the air around the barn was competitive enough without having to compare jumping skills in every lesson. Max had also decided to lighten things up by pairing the "senior" riders—students in The Saddle Club's age group—with juniors to work on position in the saddle, one of the most important parts of equitation. The younger kids always seemed to have a good time, and their ponies were so cute that the older riders loved working with them.

Lisa was paired with May Grover, a girl whom she knew from a previous junior/senior matchup. May, a skilled rider for her age, rode a pony named Macaroni. May was so enthusiastic that Lisa always enjoyed working with her.

Once everyone was paired up, Max put them through a bunch of drills, making them critique one another. Then he let them ride on their own while he watched. The lesson proceeded without incident until

Veronica collided with her own partner and screamed at her for not looking where she was going. Little Laura Heiss, who was only six, screamed right back until she was blue in the face.

Finally, Max called a halt to the argument as well as to the class. He gave them a quick pep talk for Saturday, reminding them to treat the judges with respect.

"Do we have to look perfect, Max?" May Grover asked.

"Not perfect—but pretty close to perfect, May. I expect everyone to be well groomed," Max replied, turning to go. "And that goes for you and your horses!" he called back over his shoulder. The Saddle Club looked at Carole and grinned. On more than one occasion, she had been known to show up with a beautifully turned-out horse, but with her own hair going every which way, smears of dirt on her face, and a hole or two in her breeches.

"Don't worry," Carole said tolerantly. "I promise to hose myself down before the meeting. Okay?"

May tugged on Lisa's sleeve. "I'm not sure I can get my girth tight enough by myself," she said. May's was a common problem among young riders who rode ponies. The young riders weren't as strong as the older riders, and the ponies were usually a lot fatter—and

49

better at bloating—than the horses. The combination could make girth tightening a real worry.

Lisa was wondering what advice she could offer when Stevie spoke up. "Don't worry, May," Stevie assured the girl. "I already told Jasmine James I'd get here early to help her tack up her pony, Outlaw, so I can help you, too."

"Aren't we the perfect Pony Clubber," Veronica said, her voice saccharine sweet.

"Why, thank you, Veronica," Stevie responded, pretending not to notice the sarcasm.

"Too bad brownnosing won't help you win next weekend," Veronica snapped.

Stevie said nothing—just glared, trying to think of something equally rude to answer with.

Turning her back to the group, Veronica began to sing "La Marseillaise," the French national anthem, in a loud voice. Stevie gritted her teeth. Everyone else probably thought Veronica was being weird, but Stevie knew that she was using the song to gloat. The girls were supposed to memorize the words to it for French class. Veronica had obviously finished her homework already and knew that that would annoy Stevie—who usually did her homework late—no end.

Before things could heat up any more between the two girls, Carole interrupted. She told Stevie to hurry and dismount because they had things to talk about. Reluctantly, Stevie hopped off. She was visibly seething.

On their way into the stable, Lisa suggested having a quick Saddle Club meeting at T.D.'s, the local ice-cream shop where the three of them were regulars. She wanted to plan a few more extra jumping practices.

"Sorry, can't," Stevie said. "I just remembered that I have to go do my French homework."

"French homework? Instead of ice-cream sundaes?" Lisa asked. She couldn't remember the last time Stevie had passed up—well, *anything*—in order to do homework.

Stevie nodded gravely. "Yup. Until I heard Veronica singing I forgot that we're supposed to memorize the words to 'La Marseillaise' for class tomorrow. Since Veronica obviously already knows one verse, I'm going to have to learn two verses so that I can be ahead of her."

For the second time that afternoon, Lisa and Carole found themselves shaking their heads at Stevie's competitiveness. It was incredible how far she would take things.

Stevie, however, didn't seem to find anything strange. "You guys go ahead without me," she told her friends. "And about extra practice, how about tomorrow afternoon? If Veronica shows up, we can scare her off with our great equitation over fences. Okay, Lisa? Does that sound good to you?" Without waiting for an answer, Stevie strode off with Belle, mumbling to herself in French.

Lisa didn't bother to remind her friend that scaring off Veronica wasn't *her* personal goal for the schooling show.

6

ON SATURDAY MORNING, Pine Hollow was buzzing with activity. Remembering Max's encouragement to look smart for the judges, a number of Pony Clubbers had arrived early to do an extra-good grooming job. Max and Mrs. Reg were on hand to help out anyone who needed it. They hurried from tack room to locker room to the stalls getting ready for the judges' arrival. Whenever anyone from the local horsey community visited Pine Hollow, the Regnerys wanted their farm in tip-top shape. It was part of what gave the stable one of the best reputations in Virginia.

On their way into the barn, Carole and Lisa met in

the driveway. Each was carrying her own pair of tall black dress boots.

"How late were you up polishing?" Lisa asked, noting the sheen on Carole's boots.

Carole grinned sheepishly. "To be honest, these super-shiny boots are thanks to the U.S. Marine Corps. Dad did them last night so I could go to bed early," she confessed.

Lisa sighed. "Maybe I should join the armed forces sometime so that I can learn to shine my boots that well. These just aren't as good."

"Nah," Carole told her, holding the stable door as they went inside, "you wouldn't want to do that. You wouldn't want to waste all that time on the other stuff —like marching, saluting, bed making—"

"You're right," Lisa interrupted with a grin. "Forget I even mentioned it."

Together the two girls changed and groomed Prancer and Starlight. After a while, they noticed that Stevie still hadn't shown up. They were just about to ask Max if he had heard anything, when Stevie appeared leading Belle. Stevie was perfectly dressed, and Belle's dark coat and her tack were practically glowing with cleanliness. Even her hooves, which Stevie had painted with hoof polish, looked smart. It was clear from the pair's appearance that Stevie had arrived at Pine Hollow long before Carole and Lisa had.

"So you are here, after all," Carole remarked.

"Yeah, we thought you were going to be late, but it looks like you got the early-bird prize," Lisa said. She was surprised that Stevie had beaten them to the stable.

"Oh, I've been here almost two hours," Stevie said airily. "I promised to help some of the little kids before the meeting started."

As if on cue, May Grover and Jasmine James ran up and gave Stevie a hug to thank her. They looked neat and ready for the event in their jodhpurs and paddock boots.

"I could never have gotten my girth tightened without you," May said. "Thanks, Stevie."

"Me, either," agreed Jasmine. "You're the best."

With a smile, Stevie sent the two of them on their way, promising to give them one last check before the meeting started. To Carole and Lisa she added, "I'd better give myself a once-over, too, so I'll see you two in the indoor."

Now that she thought about it, Lisa did remember Stevie's mentioning that she was going to come early. It was very un-Stevian to be anywhere early for anything, but maybe she was turning over a new leaf.

After all, she had put in extra practice without complaining at all and had been spending more time on her homework, too. Lisa voiced her thoughts to Carole as they finished tacking up.

"That's true," Carole said, "but I just hope turning over her 'new leaf' doesn't mean trying even harder to beat Veronica at all costs."

That was all the time they had to discuss Stevie's behavior for, out of the corner of her eye, Lisa saw two men and a woman dressed in horsey clothes approaching. They were talking about the rules for the upcoming schooling show. There was no question who they were: clearly, the judges had arrived. No one would dare be caught late or unprepared, especially not The Saddle Club.

To BEGIN THE mounted meeting, Max announced over the P.A. system that the judges wished to have all the riders walk their horses into the ring so that they could examine everyone's turnout. There would be no nit-picking inspections; they just wanted to meet next weekend's competitors and familiarize themselves with the different horse/rider pairs. One by one, Max's students led their mounts out until twenty gleaming horses and ponies were standing quietly, awaiting inspection.

Carole could see by the sparkle in his eye that Max was proud of their appearance. She felt proud, too—of Pine Hollow, of Starlight, and of herself. For her, the schooling show would be a perfect chance to show what she and Starlight did best. She felt confident she would reach the goal she had written down. She told as much to the judges when they began making their rounds.

"It's nice to hear someone say that enjoyment is one of their goals. There's no point in riding if it's not, is there?" one of the men asked.

"No, sir," Carole replied smartly. The three judges nodded approvingly, leaving her with a happy glow.

If anything, Lisa was even more excited than Carole at meeting the judges. When they spoke to her, they were nice and encouraging—not fierce at all. They listened attentively as she explained how young and green Prancer was, and then offered a couple of tips for helping both Prancer and Lisa to relax. By the end of the inspection, Lisa felt totally at ease. She had sort of been dreading this preliminary meeting, but now she was convinced it had been one of Max's great ideas.

As she led Prancer away, she overheard the three of them telling Max how impressed they were with the level of knowledge at Pine Hollow, as well as the excellent condition of the horses. Lisa immediately whispered the news to Carole, who whispered to May, who told Betsy Cavanaugh. Pretty soon, everyone knew and was talking excitedly. It wasn't often that they got to show off Pine Hollow all together, and it was a treat to hear that horse show judges found it as wonderful as they did.

When the riders had finished meeting with the judges, they went to await further instructions at the far end of the ring. Or, at least, most of them did. Veronica remained in the middle, holding Garnet and talking animatedly with the female judge. The Saddle Club cringed when they heard her laughing at something the judge had said.

"And she accused *me* of apple-polishing!" Stevie muttered under her breath, scowling. "Look at her—she's trying to get on that judge's good side. Not that it's a surprise, considering that it's Veronica, but I would think she'd at least be a little less obvious about it!"

Lisa and Carole shook their heads. It was definitely a revolting sight to watch Veronica falling all over the female judge. A buzz of disgruntled complaints went through the Pony Clubbers.

As if reading their minds, Max came forward and began speaking earnestly to the group. "Some of you seem surprised that Mrs. Gorham and Veronica know each other. Well—"

"You mean they know each other from before?" May piped up.

Max nodded. "Mrs. Gorham happens to belong to Mrs. diAngelo's bridge club. But there's no point in making a fuss about it. Any one of you could have known any one of the judges. Judges are human: they have friends and families and social lives. The important thing to remember is that they know their stuff, and they'll judge fairly. Got it?"

The group nodded. They knew that Max wouldn't allow any behavior that was unsportsmanlike and that his little speech was a warning to them.

Finally the judges gave the command to mount up. Everyone stopped talking, except for Veronica, who continued to make small talk with Mrs. Gorham.

"And how's your son?" she asked, putting her foot into the stirrup.

"He's quite well, thank you," the judge answered, watching Veronica grab the pommel of the saddle and begin to hoist herself up. She started to swing her right leg over Garnet's rump. Then something happened. All of a sudden, Veronica shrieked and fell to the ground.

As a unit, The Saddle Club turned to see what the

matter was. Garnet had bolted at the loud noise, Mrs. Gorham was staring, speechless, and Veronica was on the ground and had started to cry hysterically. There was a rip all the way up one side of her breeches.

As she was prone to do in an emergency, Mrs. Reg appeared out of nowhere, first-aid kit in hand. While she comforted Veronica, Max sprang into action. Telling the other riders to sit tight, he caught Garnet in a flash. Then he joined his mother at Veronica's side. By now the weeping girl had sat up. She was holding her hands to her chin, which was a bloody mess.

"What happened, Veronica?" Mrs. Reg asked.

Veronica wailed, "I c-cut my chin when I fell. I think I b-banged it on the stirrup iron."

"Her stirrup leather—it just broke in two," the judge added in a shocked voice.

Max raised his eyebrows. Carole noticed the surprised look on his face. A stirrup leather snapping was almost unheard of. In order for one to break, the leather had to be very old or neglected. It wasn't something that was easy to miss when you cleaned your tack. *If* you ever cleaned your tack, Carole thought ruefully. It was a major embarrassment to Max and to Pine Hollow that someone—Veronica— could have been that careless about routine safety.

The other two judges seemed to think so, too. Carole grimaced when she heard the clear disapproval in their voices. "Imagine not noticing a worn-out stirrup leather," one was saying.

"It is odd, especially in a group of horses that are so well turned out, to find that someone has been neglecting her tack completely," the other replied.

Carole glanced worriedly at Max to see if he had overheard the conversation, as well. His pained expression confirmed that he had. Even though it was Veronica who had made the mistake, Carole felt bad because Max looked so upset.

Stevie barely noticed Max. Instead she was focused on Veronica. Under her breath, she murmured to Lisa and Carole, "Veronica would never notice what shape her tack is in—she hardly ever even puts on her own saddle. Today, when I was finished with May and Jasmine, she asked me to help tighten *her* girth!"

Carole and Lisa smiled wanly. Somehow neither of them felt like making fun of Veronica right then. "At least she's stopped crying," Lisa pointed out, trying to be optimistic.

Veronica had indeed curbed her tears for the time being. In fact, she was glaring angrily at the judges as Mrs. Reg cleaned and bandaged her chin. Obviously, she had overheard their conversation, too, and she didn't like it one bit. Anyone who knew Veronica

could guess why she looked so peeved: she had finally
—and legitimately—gotten her chance to be the cen-
ter of everyone's attention. Instead of people pitying
her, however, they were criticizing her for her care-
lessness—and most importantly, so were the judges.

After finishing her bandaging job, Mrs. Reg pro-
nounced her medical evaluation. The cut was bleed-
ing quite hard, as often happened with cuts under the
chin. Mrs. Reg thought it would be fine, but she didn't
want to take any risks. She wanted Veronica to go to
the hospital in case she needed a couple of stitches.
At the word "stitches," Veronica burst into tears
again.

Max had been holding Garnet nearby. Now he
brought the Arabian over to her owner. In a gentle
voice, he reminded Veronica that the stable policy
was that no matter why somebody fell off a horse, they
had to get back on if they were physically able. "You
don't have to ride very far, but I do want you to get on
and take Garnet a few steps."

"I'll t-try," Veronica blubbered, "b-but how am I
s-supposed to get on without a s-stirrup leather?"

"Oh, please!" muttered Stevie. "Anybody should
be able to get on without a stirrup. What if you were
out in the woods and something broke? What would

you do then—hang around waiting for your groom to show up and hoist you on?"

In spite of themselves, Carole and Lisa started giggling. The image of Veronica's hopping around in the woods screaming for Red O'Malley to give her a leg up was too funny not to laugh.

Other riders seemed to have had enough of the Stevie/Veronica rivalry, though. When Lisa noticed the dirty looks a few people were giving The Saddle Club—and especially Stevie—she pasted a sympathetic look on her face and motioned for her two friends to do the same. Knowing Veronica, she doubted the fall was as serious as Veronica's screech implied, but this was obviously no time to point that out.

Max told Veronica he would give her a leg up. First he wanted to remove the broken leather so it wouldn't be in the way. He lifted the skirt of the saddle and pulled it out. Then he peered at the leather carefully.

Carole edged Starlight closer to the scene and looked over Max's shoulder. Like most of Veronica's tack, the leather didn't even look used, let alone worn. In fact, it was in perfect, supple shape—hardly a candidate for ripping the way everyone had seen it rip.

Max shook his head as he held up the torn ends of

the leather. Now everyone could see the terrible truth. The leather hadn't just ripped. It had been deliberately severed.

Carole let out an audible gasp. Someone had tried to sabotage Veronica!

"Of all the dirty tricks to pull!" Max exclaimed, looking stunned at first, and then angry. When he uttered his next words his voice was hard and icy. "I would like to know who, in my stable, could have done a thing like this."

At that instant, all the members of Horse Wise looked right at one person: Stevie Lake.

IT TOOK ABOUT twenty seconds for Veronica to get over the initial shock of Max's finding. After that she shrieked and screamed so loudly that half the horses in the ring shied at the sound.

"Dear, try to calm—" Mrs. Reg began.

"I can't! I can't calm down! This is completely unfair! It's the worst thing that's ever happened to me! Who could have done this to me? Why me? Why *me?!*" Veronica cried.

After letting her sob for a few minutes, Mrs. Reg took Veronica firmly by the arm. "I know you're upset, dear, but right now, you need to go to a doctor—no ifs, ands, or buts. I'm going to go get the car and take you over to the emergency room."

That said, Max fired off a set of instructions. He seemed to have decided that making Veronica ride when she was so hysterical would do more harm than good. May and Jasmine were to help Veronica to the driveway. Red O'Malley was to call Mrs. diAngelo and have her meet them at the hospital. Simon Atherton and Polly Giacomin were to put Garnet away.

Simon, who had had a crush on Veronica for some time, raced over to the horse. "We'll do our best to complete the task you ask of us in the face of this dire and shocking emergency, Max," he vowed solemnly.

The other students, who had gathered at the end of the ring, began to come forward a few at a time to tell Veronica how sorry they were. A couple of them shot dirty looks at Stevie. No one had actually come right out and said that Stevie had done it, but a lot of people were clearly thinking it. Everybody knew how badly Stevie wanted to beat Veronica, and everybody knew Stevie was famous for her practical jokes—especially when they were *im*practical.

Carole and Lisa looked around awkwardly. They didn't want to talk to anyone—not even each other. When they stole a glance at Stevie, they saw her sitting defiantly aboard Belle, purposefully ignoring the group gathered around Veronica.

Finally, Veronica headed out to the driveway with May and Jasmine. The riders left behind fell into a couple of small groups, talking earnestly in low tones. Only The Saddle Club remained silent. Lisa fidgeted with her reins. Carole rubbed at an imaginary spot on her saddle. Stevie just stared stonily at the ground.

"What's all this?" Max demanded. He had been conferring with the judges outside the ring. "Why is everyone standing around?" All at once, he began barking commands at everyone again. "What are you all waiting for? Come on, we've got a Pony Club lesson to finish—unless, of course, any of you are thinking of dropping out of the show. Start warming up—and I mean now."

Sluggishly the remaining riders organized themselves and headed out to the rail. "But Max, what about Veronica?" Betsy Cavanaugh asked.

"What about her? She's being taken to the Willow Creek hospital. I'm sure she'll be fine," Max replied.

"But her stirrup leather was—" Polly Giacomin started to say, her eyes on Stevie.

"Polly, did you hear me say 'Start warming up'? Because it looks like you're standing still," Max commented drily.

* * *

BEFORE LONG, THE Pony Clubbers had snapped back to attention. They warmed up and prepared for the mock competition. The judges seemed a bit skeptical about carrying on as if nothing had happened, but they followed Max's lead. By the time the course was set up, everything was almost back to normal. It was funny, though, hardly any of the students rode as well as they had in practice. The bad feeling that Veronica's fall had generated was hanging over the whole stable.

Stevie and Carole managed to do fairly well. Both got around the course without incident, although there was something lackluster about their performances. Belle didn't have the flair over fences that she had shown on Tuesday, and Starlight didn't even try to get strong. He almost seemed bored.

Lisa wasn't as lucky as her friends. All morning she had been looking forward to her ride, eager to prove how much the extra practices had helped Prancer and her. But now the incident with Veronica weighed heavily on her mind. As she headed toward the first jump, a low brush fence, all her confidence drained away. She felt Prancer hesitate. She knew that the horse just needed a strong reminder to keep going forward, but for some reason, Lisa got scared. She dropped her hands and fell forward on Prancer's neck right before the fence.

This time, instead of jumping anyway, Prancer stopped. Lisa could hardly believe it—a refusal! And at the first fence!

Yet there was a part of Lisa that felt as if she deserved a refusal. She couldn't expect Prancer to keep saving her when she messed up. An old school horse might have packed her around, but not a young Thoroughbred. What was wrong with her all of a sudden? It felt as if she had unlearned everything she had worked on so hard. Everyone would think she was hopeless. She glanced anxiously at Max as she made a circle to approach the jump again.

Because it was supposed to be a mock competition, Max had told them that he would not intervene unless absolutely necessary. After Prancer's second refusal, though, he came forward to help. Lisa's face flamed red with embarrassment. She was the first person all morning to need Max's help. Of course what he told her were things she knew already: eyes up, sit firmly, don't drop your hands right before the fence.

It was even more embarrassing when Max dropped the top poles of the second and third fences to the ground, lowering the jumps about six inches to make them more inviting. On her third approach, Lisa repeated Max's words to herself. This time, she got over it and continued around the rest of the course. The whole thing felt messy and uncomfortable, though, and she knew she wasn't in sync with Prancer.

When she pulled up at the end of the ring, she was flustered and angry. Instead of talking with the others, as the previous riders had done, she went to walk Prancer by herself. At the moment, she couldn't face anyone, not even Stevie and Carole. As she led Prancer away, she flashed back to the other morning when Mrs. Reg had told that silly story about the stable witch and the boy who got spooked every time he attempted the cross-country course. Am I being jinxed, too? she wondered.

Come on, Lisa, she told herself a moment later. That was just a dumb story.

RUBBING DOWN STARLIGHT after the meeting, Carole debated with herself. Her friends' troubles were all she could think about. Should she come right out and say, "Listen, Lisa, it's obvious you're still having problems with Prancer, but I *know* you can fix them by next weekend"?

And what about the Veronica situation? So far Stevie hadn't said very much about the fact that everyone thought she was the one who had sabotaged Veronica. Should Carole bring it up?

A moment later Carole sighed. If she were the one who had ridden poorly, she would hardly want her friends to mention it. And if she had been the one who was under suspicion, she would expect The Saddle Club, above everyone else, to believe in her innocence.

Slowly Carole thought back over Veronica's fall. It irked her to think of how quickly everyone had jumped to conclusions about Stevie. Of course, Stevie's rivalry with Veronica had been escalating all week, which made the situation even worse. Everyone had probably overheard at least one of Stevie's disparaging remarks about Veronica. So everyone, naturally, had turned to Stevie as the scapegoat.

But for Carole it was different. She *knew* Stevie. Stevie was one of her best friends. And Carole could no sooner believe that Stevie had slit the stirrup leather than believe that she had slit it herself. But then, the question remained, who had?

Starlight blew through his nostrils, interrupting his owner's thoughts. Carole shook her head in puzzlement and wished aloud, for probably the thousandth time in her life, "Why can't people be more like horses?"

After thinking things over some more, she arrived at what she determined was a safe decision: a Saddle Club meeting at T.D.'s—pronto.

Lisa and Stevie said they were game. The three of them finished grooming, helped Red with the afternoon haying and watering, and convened in the driveway. Too late, they noticed the Pine Hollow station wagon returning from the hospital. All three of them were eager to avoid a run-in with Veronica. They hung back while the other riders and the judges ran over and surrounded the car. Veronica emerged, wearing a bulky bandage on her chin. Her face was red, and her eyes were swollen from crying.

"You poor dear, how are you feeling?" Mrs. Gorham inquired. She put a comforting arm around Veronica's shoulder.

Before Veronica could answer, the rest of the group began clamoring for her attention.

"How many stitches did you have to get?" asked Jasmine.

"Are you in a lot of pain?" Simon wanted to know.

"What did the doctor say?"

"Can you still ride?"

"Are you going to get back on Garnet?"

When the barrage of questions finally ended, Veronica began to speak. She put on a brave front but was clearly upset and very close to crying again. "I'm not sure if I'll be able to jump next weekend," she said gravely. "It's not as if I broke my leg or anything, but my cut is throbbing pretty badly. I don't know if I could take the jostling over the jumps. Besides, I bruised my knee and calf on the stirrup iron."

"Of all the horrible things to happen," Mrs. Gorham said. "I'm sure your mother was terribly shaken."

Veronica nodded. "Yes, Mrs. Gorham, she really was. Most of all, she couldn't believe someone would do this to me." Veronica paused and let her eyes rest suggestively on The Saddle Club. After a sniff, she continued, "She didn't want me to come back here, but I know I have to get back on a horse today. For now, I'll walk a little. And I'll just have to wait and see if I can make it next week."

A sympathetic murmur went up from the crowd. Half a dozen Pony Clubbers volunteered to tack up Garnet again. Another bunch helped Veronica limp into the stable. She went slowly, favoring her bruised leg.

The Saddle Club watched her go. Carole and Lisa felt a twinge of sympathy. They knew Veronica well enough to realize that she was enjoying all the attention, but it seemed mean to even think about that.

The fact was, she was hurt and might have to miss the show. It would be a hard thing for anyone to take.

When Lisa glanced at Stevie, she noticed that their friend still didn't share their sympathy. Her face showed nothing but disdain. If anything, she was scowling harder now than in the ring.

"What are you guys looking at?" she asked Carole and Lisa bluntly. "Do you honestly think I care whether Veronica can 'make it' next weekend?"

"Stevie," Carole began timidly, "aren't you at all sorry for her?"

"Hardly," Stevie retorted, her face flushed. "How can I be? Veronica's blaming me for cutting her stirrup leather. I had nothing to do with it. So why should I pretend to care who did?"

Carole didn't have an easy answer for Stevie. But she did know that it was crucial that the three of them get to T.D.'s—and fast. That way, they could sort out the day's events and devise a plan for sticking together through the next few days, days that were sure to be an ordeal for them if Veronica had her way.

T.D.'s WAS BUSIER than usual, even for a Saturday afternoon. One look around, and it was easy to tell why. The Saddle Club weren't the only ones who had had the idea to adjourn to the ice-cream shop to discuss the morning's events. A number of tables were filled with other Horse Wise members. The whole contingent who had come over from Pine Hollow looked up when Carole, Lisa, and Stevie entered. Carole and Lisa couldn't help but glance at Stevie to see how she would react.

Stevie took one look around, jutted out her chin defiantly, and glared right back at every table of Pine Hollow riders. Then she headed purposefully toward

The Saddle Club's usual booth, where she sat down and began reading the menu intently.

Carole and Lisa followed, feeling terrible. They wanted to seem as confident as Stevie; instead they felt as guilty as criminals.

After Stevie had ordered, she got up to go to the ladies' room, and Carole and Lisa held a quick consultation. Naturally, both of them wanted more than anything to believe that their best friend was innocent.

"We have to look at the evidence, though," Lisa pointed out in a worried tone. "Stevie *is* the world's biggest practical joker. This is the girl who gave us plaster of paris instead of pancakes. From the day I met Stevie, she's always had a trick up her sleeve." Lisa was thinking back to her first lesson at Pine Hollow when Stevie had taken the stirrups off of Lisa's saddle. When she went to mount, it was impossible.

At the time, Lisa hadn't thought the joke was very humorous. But as soon as she had gotten to know Stevie, she had realized that the prank was Stevie's idea of a harmless good time. Since then, there had been a number of Stevie Lake "classics"—boot swapping, horse swapping, the works. And Lisa had laughed right along with everyone else at the results—or even taken part in the setup. This time, though, the joke wasn't very funny, nor had Stevie mentioned a word about it to her friends.

"Stevie does go pretty far sometimes, but isn't slashing someone's stirrup leather a bit more than a practical joke?" Carole asked. She had been thinking of Stevie's past escapades, too. Not one of them came even close to slashing someone's leathers so that the rider would fall off a horse.

"Maybe she figured Veronica would see it right away," Lisa reasoned, "or that the judges would find it and criticize Veronica during her inspection. Then Veronica would have either had to admit she didn't clean her own tack, or take the blame for missing such an obvious problem when she did clean it." Lisa paused. "You and I both know that nothing would give Stevie more pleasure than watching Veronica make a fool out of herself a week before the show. Heck, except for Simon Atherton, every one of us was probably hoping that she'd trip herself up somehow so that the judges would see what a spoiled brat she is."

"You're right. And it was just a fluke that the judges didn't inspect us more carefully. If they had, we all would have thought it served Veronica right," Carole admitted.

Lisa nodded. "Besides, everyone knows how badly

Stevie wanted to beat Veronica. It doesn't look good for her, Carole."

"I know," Carole replied glumly. "I keep thinking about how she suddenly decided to lend a helping hand to the younger kids—"

"And so she was at the stable unusually early," Lisa finished.

"She even tightened Veronica's girth for her," Carole said.

"Right, but Veronica did ask her to," Lisa said.

"Or at least Stevie told us that Veronica asked her to," Carole said. She and Lisa exchanged heartsick glances. It felt terrible to be talking like this. They were practically putting their friend on trial. When the waitress arrived with their ice creams, they couldn't touch them. Even the sight of Stevie's typically outrageous sundae failed to cheer them up.

"Hey, let's dig in," Stevie said enthusiastically, rejoining the table. She picked up her spoon and was about to take a big bite out of the multicolored ice cream and topping mound. As she raised the spoon to her lips, she paused, meeting Lisa's and Carole's eyes. One look at their faces and she lost her appetite at once. She set her spoon down with a clatter. Her mind was reeling. Were her best friends turning on her, too? Was it something she had said? She knew that she'd been pretty harsh on Veronica, but that was nothing new.

"Listen, you guys," Stevie began. She paused to get control of her voice which had started to quaver.

As Stevie searched for the right words, a stir went through the restaurant. The Saddle Club looked toward the door. Veronica had come in and was standing at the entrance scanning the crowd. Finally her eyes rested on their table. The look on her face said it all. She had come to make Stevie pay.

In the hush that fell, the only sound was the angry tap of Veronica's shoes as she marched toward them, hands on her hips. She stopped before The Saddle Club's booth and took a deep breath. Everyone waited for her to erupt.

But before she could say a word, Stevie sprang up. She looked Veronica straight in the eye. Her voice had stopped shaking completely. "You are going to be very sorry if you make any kind of an accusation about anything at all," she warned, loudly enough for the whole restaurant to hear. "In case you've forgotten, my mother and father are lawyers. If you start telling stories about me, I'll slap a lawsuit on you so fast you'll wish you lived in Abu Dhabi!"

Veronica's jaw snapped shut. Stevie's threat had rendered her speechless. There was nothing left for

Veronica to do but back down for the time being, and she knew it. She turned on her heel and marched out. A few Horse Wise members followed, calling after her to wait up. The Saddle Club stared after the retreating group.

"Well," Stevie said, "that might have kept her from talking, but it sure didn't make her change her mind about me. I know she still thinks I did it. And the chances of my parents agreeing to get involved in this mess are about one in a million." With an exasperated sigh, Stevie sat back down in the booth, and looked at her friends.

Carole and Lisa were staring at her in silence. Tears gathered in Stevie's eyes as she stood up again, this time to face her best friends. "I can take anything from Veronica," she said in a choked voice. "But I can't stand my two best friends in the world doubting me!"

Carole and Lisa didn't try to stop Stevie as she hastily tossed money onto the table and fled from the restaurant. Both of them knew that it was no use. The only thing they could say was that she was right— they were doubting her. They slumped in their booth, staring at Stevie's dripping sundae as if it, somehow, held the answer.

9

IN SPITE OF all that had happened, Lisa hadn't forgotten her goal for the schooling show. She had decided to work hard both at Pine Hollow and at home. That night she wrote out yet another list of things she had to work on with Prancer.

When her alarm sounded the next morning, she flicked on her light and studied the list to remind herself of all of her problems. "Things I Need to Do in Order to Jump Better" was its title. So far it read:

1. Keep eyes up.
2. Keep heels down.
3. Don't lean too far forward.

4.   Don't lean too far back.
5.   Don't drop reins before the fence.
6.   Don't hang on reins over the fence.
7.   Don't rise up too high in saddle.
8.   Don't sit too low in saddle.
9.   Don't stiffen up.
10.   Don't get nervous.
11.   Don't be tense.
12.   Don't worry about anything.

Lisa wasn't exactly sure how she was going to concentrate on numbers 1 through 8 without forgetting
about numbers 9 through 12, but she figured that
would work itself out.

She got a ride over to Pine Hollow from her
mother. The whole way there, she studied the list until she knew it backward and forward. She had wanted
to consult with Carole or Stevie about it, but it
seemed insensitive to be worrying about her jumping
position when Stevie's whole future at Pine Hollow
was on the line. Besides, who knew if Stevie was even
talking to Carole and her. She'd been so upset when
she left T.D.'s yesterday.

Lisa could hardly believe her eyes when her
mother's station wagon pulled into the driveway at

Pine Hollow. Veronica was there, riding Garnet over the outside course as if yesterday had never happened.

Lisa had her mother stop the car next to the ring so she could get out. There were a couple of questions she wanted to ask Veronica—like how she was able to ride with her supposedly "throbbing" cut, and how she had managed to recover so quickly. Lisa couldn't wait to tell Stevie and Carole about Veronica's being here.

To Lisa's frustration, Veronica pretended not to notice her standing at the rail, despite Lisa's calls and waves. "I won't be so easy to miss when I'm on a bigger horse than yours," Lisa muttered.

When she returned to the ring fifteen minutes later, mounted on Prancer, Veronica trotted over to say hello. "Back for some more schooling, Lisa? I'll be happy to help you out again," Veronica volunteered sweetly. "I'm sure you're making a lot of progress with what we went over last week."

Lisa bit her lip hard to keep from snapping back. If she wanted to check out Veronica's physical condition so that she could report back to The Saddle Club, she was going to have to put up with her fake sweetness and obnoxious comments. "Yeah, I thought we could use some more practice. I guess you were thinking the same thing?" she inquired.

"Obviously. Yesterday was a complete loss for Garnet and me. The rest of you had the advantage of riding in front of the judges, whereas I spent the morning in the emergency room," Veronica replied with a sniff. "I'll be lucky if I can catch up."

Lisa smiled tentatively. "It sure is great that you're recovering so fast," she said.

Veronica glowered, obviously taking Lisa's comment for a sarcastic remark. In a split second, she completely dropped the nice act and spat out, "No thanks to your practical joking friend! If I wanted to, I'm the one who could sue! I could have been hurt a lot worse. I was lucky to escape with a few stitches and a couple of bruises. This time, Stevie Lake has gone too far—*way* too far. Everyone says so. I'll bet she even feels guilty about what she's done. I'll bet if she could go back, she would never have put me at risk that way! You should thank your lucky stars I'm back riding today!" Veronica finished her attack in a high-pitched shriek.

Lisa had kept her mouth shut during the tirade. She didn't know what to think, and even if she had, she wasn't about to share it with Veronica. Being one of Stevie's best friends, she was already more involved in the mess than she wanted to be. Still, it was interesting to see how defensively Veronica had reacted to her simple question about recovering. It was clear that she knew how bad it looked to be back riding one day after the dramatic scene she had made.

The worst part about meeting up with Veronica was that now Lisa was stuck riding with her. At first, she actually felt glad for the opportunity to prove herself to Veronica. She was tired of feeling that everyone doubted her ability, and this would be the perfect chance to redeem herself and Prancer—or so she thought.

All too soon, however, she realized that the morning was going to be a repeat of their previous session. Veronica did fine although, Lisa told herself, not as well as Stevie or Carole would have done. She still looked flashy as opposed to confident. At any rate, her cut didn't seem to be bothering her or affecting her riding at all.

For some reason, though, Lisa simply could not get herself together. The more "help" Veronica gave her, the worse she did. She felt discombobulated, couldn't concentrate, and had several refusals. The thought of her list of problems only discouraged her further. Veronica stood in the middle of the ring, making a zillion suggestions all at once. "Sit deeper! Don't lean that far forward! And watch your elbows! Don't forget to release in midair! Look up! Now look for your next fence!"

Lisa tried to swallow her pride and listen, but it was all she could do to stop from screaming with frustration. She *knew* everything Veronica was saying, she just couldn't do it all at once. Today she could hardly do any of it.

The only reprieve came when Veronica finally got her fill of lecturing and headed in. By that point, Lisa was so worked up that she just rode on the flat for a few minutes, trying to salvage some small success for the morning. Even riding alone didn't do the trick this time, though. Finally she let Prancer walk on a loose rein. Again and again she went over her efforts to improve, wondering what on earth could have gone so terribly wrong in the past few sessions. When she went to dismount, Lisa was convinced that she was riding and jumping worse than the day she had started at Pine Hollow.

Totally discouraged, she put Prancer away and went to change in the locker room. Veronica was inside changing, too. She immediately jumped on Lisa with a ton of suggestions. Lisa nodded blankly from time to time. Sheer exhaustion kept her from telling Veronica not to bother, that she couldn't absorb another riding tip in a million years.

"And so if you work really hard for the next few days, you'll have a chance of getting around the course. I'm sure of it," Veronica concluded with a condescending smile. She finished tying her tennis shoe and stood up, picking up her bag. As she rose, something long and gray fell out of the bag. Whatever it was landed near Lisa, who reached down automatically to pick it up. Before she could grab it, though, Veronica shoved past her to get to it first. In the process, she accidentally kicked the object under the row of lockers, out of reach. Lisa gave her a questioning look.

"Oh, it's nothing," Veronica said, shrugging off Lisa's curiosity. "Just something I picked up at the beauty parlor. Now, I'd better scoot. I have to go breeches shopping today." With that, she picked up the pair she had been wearing when she fell. The tear went straight up the leg, so it was clear that they really weren't reparable.

"It's a good thing I was wearing my oldest pair," Veronica went on. "I hate to think of how mad Mother would have been if I'd wrecked one of my European pairs. At least these are replaceable," she added, dropping the breeches into the garbage and walking out.

Lisa wasn't sorry to see her leave. In fact, being

alone in the locker room was such a relief that she lay down on the bench to think for a minute or two. As she lay there with her eyes closed, she thought about the morning's horrible practice. Although it had been very, very disappointing, Lisa was still far from wanting to give up. She planned her next practice in her mind, visualizing the jumps. Her eyes would be up; her hands would be steady. . . .

Opening her eyes a few minutes later, Lisa found herself staring at the gray object underneath the lockers. Why had Veronica tried to get it so quickly? Lisa got down on her hands and knees and felt for it, but it was out of reach.

Suddenly Lisa felt a bit foolish. What would she say if Mrs. Reg walked in? Yesterday it had seemed as if everyone at Pine Hollow felt sorry for Veronica. Mrs. Reg would hardly tolerate any nonsense that involved her, especially if it came from a member of The Saddle Club. This time, Lisa decided, she would have to do as her mother always suggested, and let sleeping dogs lie—that is, not stick her nose into something that wasn't her concern.

On the way out, Lisa stopped by Max's office to ask him if she could work with Prancer after school the next day. Because she didn't own Prancer, Max occasionally used the horse for other students or turned her out for the afternoon. As Lisa approached his office, she noted that the door was closed—a rarity at Pine Hollow, a stable that prided itself on its welcoming, open atmosphere.

Lisa could hear Max talking on the phone, so she sat down on a hay bale to wait. Max's voice carried through the door, and before she knew it, she was listening to his end of the conversation.

"I realize that, Mrs. diAngelo," Max was saying, "but I have to be fair to all my students, not just your daughter. Right now, there's no proof that Stevie Lake was the perpetrator . . . Yes, I know you're convinced that she was, but do you really want me to bar her from the show based on a hunch? . . . I have to say it seems a bit premature . . . I can't give you a decision right away . . . Of course, of course I will punish the wrongdoer, just as soon as we find out who that is. . . ."

It was all Lisa could do to stop herself from banging through the door, wresting the phone from Max's hands, and yelling a blue streak at Veronica's mother. How dare the woman demand that Stevie be denied the right to compete in the show? The idea that Mrs. diAngelo would presume that just because someone had—

Mid-thought, Lisa paused. Just because someone

had—what? A chill went down Lisa's spine. Just because someone had slashed a stirrup leather, that was what. Just because someone had tried to sabotage Veronica. Just because, she realized, someone had risked putting both a horse and a rider in extreme danger. This was serious business. Whoever had taken that kind of risk didn't deserve the honor of competing with other riders.

But just what did that say about Stevie?

10

As FAST AS she could, Lisa gathered up her stuff and tore out of Pine Hollow. She ran toward home, her head spinning, but there was one clear thought in her mind: she just had to talk to Carole. That was her only chance of sorting through this horrible mess.

What would Stevie say when she found out that she might not be allowed to ride in the show? And what if Carole and Lisa didn't defend her to Max? Would she ever talk to them again? But what could they say to Max when they didn't know what to think themselves? Lisa ran faster and faster.

As she ran, jumbled-up bits of Max's conversation and her own thoughts floated back to her. "Have to be fair to all my students—no proof that Stevie Lake was the perpetrator—both a horse and a rider in extreme danger—extreme danger—both a horse and a rider . . ." The words ran through Lisa's head almost faster than her feet ran over the ground. Something was wrong with the picture. Something was definitely wrong, but she didn't know what. Her burning lungs forced her to slow to a jog. Why couldn't she figure out what was bothering her?

Then it came to her. *Someone had risked putting both a horse and a rider in extreme danger.* How could she have been so blind? Lisa came to a complete standstill. She stood panting by the side of the road, as her mind went over and over the evidence.

Stevie wouldn't be above doing something that would make a fool of Veronica diAngelo, any more than she'd be above serving plaster of paris pancakes or expecting Lisa to climb into a saddle without stirrups. Humans could take a knock or two and be fine. Making them look stupid was part of the joke.

But there was no way, ever, at any time, that Stevie would do something to imperil a horse. And yet, sabotaging a stirrup leather would do just that. If a leather broke in the middle of the jump, unseating the rider, the horse could become equally imbalanced. A jumping horse who took a spill could break a leg! As sure as

Lisa had brown hair and freckles, Stevie Lake was innocent.

Never had the thought of a horse's breaking its leg made Lisa so excited. She forgot all about her spent lungs. Remembering the unfair assumptions about Stevie that everyone—including her and Carole—had made spurred her on, and she sprinted flat out toward home.

Carole picked up the phone after one ring. Breathlessly, Lisa poured out her story of overhearing Mrs. diAngelo's call. "All the way home, I felt like a sleuth in a mystery story who knows she's heard enough to crack the case but just can't sort out the information. But it's simple, really. Veronica got so hysterical that everyone focused on how hurt she was. The only thing that happened to Garnet was that she got scared and ran around the ring. But think about what would have happened if the leather hadn't broken when Veronica was mounting. What if it had snapped, say, in midair, over one of the fences?"

Carole, who would rather have broken her own arm than seen Starlight with a sniffle, didn't need much more prompting than that. Her train of thought followed the same path Lisa's had, and she came to the same conclusion. "Stevie would never put Garnet at risk like that!" she cried. "She would never make the horse an innocent victim of her feud with Veronica."

"Exactly," Lisa said, relieved that Carole was now as convinced as she was of Stevie's innocence. "We forgot that cutting the leather was an attack on Garnet, too."

Now that the two girls realized that they were back on Stevie's side where they belonged, a huge weight seemed to have been lifted off them. They could hardly believe that they had truly doubted their friend. And now there was one thing they had to do and do it right away: call Stevie and apologize. It wasn't going to be fun, but both Carole and Lisa knew their friend deserved the apology.

LYING ON HER bed at home, Stevie stared up at the ceiling. She had spent practically the whole day in her room, feeling awful. There was a knot in her stomach that wouldn't go away. It was one thing to know that the biggest snob at Pine Hollow had it in for you, but it was another thing entirely when your friends betrayed you. She had seen the doubt in Lisa's and Carole's eyes, and it hurt. She couldn't believe that they, of all people, thought she was capable of such an attack. Since running out of T.D.'s, she had racked her brain trying to find a way to convince them of her innocence. But the fact was, it made her mad to have to convince them at all. If they were going to join the diAngelo camp, then nothing could stop them.

With a sigh, Stevie rolled onto her stomach, letting her left arm drop to the floor. She knew she couldn't just stay there forever. Without Saddle Club plans, though, it was hard to get motivated to do much of anything.

The shrill ringing of her bedroom phone broke through Stevie's thoughts. She had nearly fallen asleep, she was so exhausted with worry.

"Stevie, it's for you!" Mrs. Lake called.

"Who is it?" Stevie yelled back.

"Who do you think it is? It's Lisa and Carole!" Mrs. Lake answered.

Listlessly, Stevie sat up to take the call. She really didn't feel like talking to Lisa and Carole. There was nothing they could say to her that would make any difference if they were still unsure about whom to believe. And it would only make her feel worse to listen to them avoiding the subject. After a long pause she picked up the receiver. "Yes?" she said curtly. "What do you want?"

Lisa jumped right in with the story of Mrs. diAngelo. "She's really trying to persuade Max to keep you out of the show because of what happened to

Veronica. Max was defending you, but he's under a lot of pressure. He hasn't decided what to do yet, and we've been thinking—"

Before Lisa could explain the purpose of her call, Stevie broke in, furious at her friends. "Well, I've been thinking, too!" she practically yelled. "And you know what I've been thinking? That one of the rules of The Saddle Club is that we be willing to help each other out in any kind of situation. Or is that not one of the rules anymore? If you guys think I shouldn't ride in the show, fine!"

Stevie's fingers were trembling as she gripped the receiver, waiting for Carole and Lisa's reaction to her angry torrent. She hated to talk that way to her friends, but Mrs. diAngelo's attempt to keep her out of the show was the last straw. How could The Saddle Club just stand by and let it happen?

"Stevie?" Carole asked quietly.

Stevie could hardly respond. Finally she managed to get out a choked "Yes?"

"We were calling to tell you that we're sorry we ever doubted you, we believe in your innocence one hundred percent, and we'll stand behind you no matter what," Carole said.

Stevie stared at the receiver suspiciously. "But, I

don't get it—why did you change your minds?" she asked.

In a rush, Lisa and Carole explained how they had come to their conclusion. They had known that Stevie would do anything to beat Veronica—or at least almost anything. What they hadn't realized until today was that a trick like slashing the stirrup leather was just as dangerous for Garnet as for Garnet's rider.

"We know you'd never do anything that would put a horse at risk," Lisa finished.

Again there was a pause, as Stevie tried to absorb everything that her friends were saying. It was funny, but she had been so surprised that someone else seemed to have it in for Veronica, she hadn't thought of Garnet either. And now it was nice to hear her friends apologize, but the memory of yesterday still stung. These were her two best friends in the world, and their doubting her had hurt—badly. Stevie couldn't just put on a cheery face and pretend everything was perfect.

"It's nice of you to call," she said, finally. "But it would have been even nicer if you had been there for me yesterday."

"We know," Carole and Lisa responded in unison. "And you're right—the way we acted was completely out of line with The Saddle Club ideals," Lisa added.

"We'll try to make it up to you," Carole said gravely.

Stevie paused before saying, "I guess I am a little too competitive with Veronica. I can understand why you thought I might have gone overboard this time." Then, with an effort to laugh, she added, "I sure look guilty, though, don't I?"

Lisa hesitated. "I hate to say it, Stevie, but you're the obvious culprit."

Lisa and Carole went on to apologize nine or ten more times before Stevie could cut them off.

"Listen—apology accepted, okay?" she said. She knew it might take a while longer for her to completely forgive Lisa and Carole, but there was no point in making them grovel.

Now that the air was cleared, Lisa decided that it was time to get back to the practical aspect of the problem.

"I think there's only one solution," she continued. "We have to find the real perpetrator and expose him —or her—to Max."

"But that's practically impossible. Veronica has so many enemies, how can we single out one?" Stevie joked.

"With some good old-fashioned sleuthing," Lisa replied.

"Some good old-fashioned, lightning-fast sleuthing, you mean," Carole put in. "We've got to clear Stevie's name in less than a week."

"There's no better time than the present," said Lisa. "Let's get back to the scene of the crime."

The girls agreed to meet at Pine Hollow that afternoon. They would do some investigating, as well as take a Saddle Club ride together.

That prompted Stevie to ask Lisa how the jumping practices were going. Lisa sighed. "They're going nowhere fast," she said glumly. She described her torturous sessions with Veronica. "The worst thing is, she's right most of the time. I make so many mistakes that I can't even remember all of them. I wrote down a list of problems, but it's not helping. As soon as I remember one thing, I forget the other twenty-five. Poor Prancer has just about given up on me. Every time we go near a fence, I can practically feel her cringing."

Stevie and Carole were sympathetic to Lisa's problems. Both of them felt bad that they hadn't helped her out more. And both agreed that trying to learn anything from Veronica—or even in her presence— was probably next to impossible. They promised to try and help figure out what was going wrong.

"You know what?" Lisa said. "I feel better already. Somehow, when The Saddle Club works together, I feel like there's no obstacle we can't conquer."

"Or jump over," Stevie added, giggling. With a click she put down the receiver. In one phone call, her day had gone from total frustration to total relief. She was so glad that Carole and Lisa were back on her side that even the news about Mrs. diAngelo seemed unimportant.

Humming happily, she began to fish her riding stuff out of her overflowing hamper.

11

"BUT I THOUGHT I was *supposed* to lean forward," Lisa said. The three girls had set up a short course of jumps in the outside ring—nothing big, but with enough variety to bring out whatever problems Lisa felt she had. Carole and Stevie were watching Lisa go over them. Unfortunately, Lisa seemed to be getting more and more uptight as the practice session progressed.

Carole thought for a minute. "You are supposed to lean forward—just not that far forward." She didn't know how else to put it. That was the hard thing about being an instructor: you not only had to know what to do, you also had to be able to explain it in such a way that your student understood. It was part of what made teaching fun, but right now, Carole just wanted to zap the information into Lisa's brain.

On her next time around, Lisa's jumping position was better, but she was still having problems with her hands. She either dropped them completely before the fence or held on too late. Again Carole struggled for the right words, but all she could say for sure was that Lisa's timing was off. She knew Max would have been able to assess the problem in a matter of minutes and provide encouraging and useful advice.

"I can't seem to get into any kind of a rhythm," Lisa said. "I'm either ahead or behind."

"That's because you're too worried about it," Stevie told her. "You've got to relax."

Ruefully, Lisa thought of the list she had made. "I know I do, but it's like a catch twenty-two. I can't relax into a rhythm because I'm too worried about it, and I can't stop worrying until I relax." Lisa knew how frustrated she sounded, and, for once, she didn't care. At least with Carole and Stevie critiquing her, she didn't feel that she had to pretend to be pleased with her performance. Unlike Veronica, they truly wanted her to do well. Besides, they had seen her do well previously so they knew she could. But even all their help wasn't helping. Every adjustment she made seemed exaggerated and uncomfortable. She didn't want to admit it, but for the first time since she'd made her resolution, she felt like giving up.

"I'm really beginning to think I'm cursed," Lisa announced, only half kidding. "There's got to be some kind of witch jinxing my jumping."

Carole and Stevie laughed.

"I thought I heard a rusty chain clanking up in the hayloft," Stevie joked.

"How about giving it another go?" Carole suggested. To herself, she vowed to think up more creative ways to explain to Lisa what she was doing wrong.

Lisa agreed. She wasn't going to quit when Carole was volunteering so much of her time.

"I've got a better idea," Stevie said. "How about *not* giving it another go, at least for now, and taking a trail ride instead?"

"I have to confess that a trail ride sounds great," Lisa said. The thought of wandering through the woods had already brought a relieved smile to her lips.

"Count me in," Carole said. She had a feeling she knew what was behind Stevie's suggestion.

As she and Stevie went to get Starlight and Belle, who were tied to the rail, Stevie filled her in on what she'd been thinking. "Lisa is too uptight and nervous to do anything right. She needs a chance to erase all the mistakes she's made and just enjoy herself," Stevie said.

Carole looked at her with respect. Stevie had figured out a way around Lisa's problems instead of through them. Sometimes fun was the answer. Carole made a mental note to remember that with her future students, that was, if she decided to become an instructor instead of a breeder, trainer, veterinarian, or competitive rider. For now, she made a note to remember it herself.

While the two of them mounted, Lisa volunteered to go in and tell Max where they were going. It was Pine Hollow policy never to leave on a trail ride without mentioning your intended route to someone. That way, if anything happened, people would know where to start looking for you.

Max was happy to hear that they were taking a break from schooling. He told them to forget about the week's troubles and enjoy themselves. Lisa promised to do her best. When she returned to the ring, both Carole and Stevie had funny looks on their faces. Lisa figured they had been talking about her jumping problems but had stopped when they saw her, not wanting to hurt her feelings. She appreciated their concern and decided to say nothing.

Chattering happily, the three girls headed out

across the back pasture. While they loved everything about horses, there was nothing quite like the freedom of riding on a shady, well-worn trail. As soon as they turned onto it, all three of them paused to inhale the wonderful, woodsy smell. With so much on their minds lately, it was even a bigger treat than usual to be getting away on their own. Starlight, Prancer, and Belle seemed to sense their good mood. The horses walked along at a nice pace, swinging their tails and pricking up their ears at the sound of birds.

As usual, Carole was in the lead, with Lisa next, and Stevie last. Lisa followed Carole attentively. She watched the light, easy way Carole sat in the saddle and tried to imitate her position. When they began to trot, Lisa felt her own sense of rhythm start to come back. She posted along contentedly. In another few minutes she thought she might even feel like whistling.

Carole led them along the edge of a neighboring field, trotting and cantering for long stretches. When she got to the end, she veered right, onto a sort of serpentine, off the usual trail. "I've always wanted to explore back this way!" she called.

"Why not?" Lisa called back. She figured Carole was hoping to find another meadow that they could canter in. All of them felt like cantering today.

At the end of Carole's serpentine, they came to a long stone wall bordering the woods. The wall marked the edge of Pine Hollow property. The Saddle Club knew because Max was constantly reminding them to get permission if they were going to go past the stone walls. Sensibly, Carole slowed to a walk. She walked the length of the wall before turning and taking a trail straight into the woods. Then she picked up a trot again.

Once more, Lisa felt the happy sensation of being completely at one with her horse. Prancer perked up her stride and really moved. Up ahead, Carole seemed to be having an equally good time with Starlight. A couple of times, Lisa meant to turn around and check on Stevie, but she was so busy comparing her position to Carole's and so thrilled about feeling like a decent rider again that she forgot. Besides, Stevie was such a good rider that there was nothing to worry about.

Up ahead, Carole slowed once more to a walk. Lisa figured she had stopped to give Starlight a breather. Then she saw Carole halt and turn around in the saddle, staring over her shoulder, beyond Lisa. Trying to get a better look, Carole stood up in her stirrups and shielded her eyes. All at once, she started waving.

Completely confused, Lisa looked to see where Carole was pointing. Turning in her saddle, she wondered what was up with Stevie now. "If this is another practical joke, Stevie—" she began to say. She stopped when she realized that no one was listening.

Stevie was gone. There was no sign of her, as far down the trail as Lisa could see. Immediately, Lisa halted Prancer and listened. She heard a voice, faint at first, but unmistakably Stevie's. She was calling for help from her friends. But where was she?

In a split second, Lisa had her horse turned around and headed back down the trail. All she could think was that Stevie was in trouble and needed her. Images of fallen riders lying helpless on the ground flashed before Lisa's eyes. She urged Prancer into a canter, then a gallop. As they neared the end of the trail, Lisa heard Stevie again. Her voice was coming from the field that lay beyond a low gray wall.

Without hesitating, Lisa rode straight for the gray stones. She could feel Prancer confident beneath her. She leaned forward, reached forward with her hands, and rose in the saddle. They flew over the stone wall in perfect unison, landing gently on the other side.

As soon as she landed, Lisa spotted Stevie, standing in the middle of the field, holding Belle. Lisa hurried over to her, worried sick about what she would find. With every step closer she took, however, her worry got diluted: Stevie had a huge grin on her face. As

Lisa pulled to a halt beside her, she heard Starlight landing in the field. Carole cantered up next to them. If anything, her grin was bigger than Stevie's. Lisa looked from one to another incredulously.

"We knew you could do it," Stevie said.

"Do what?" Lisa asked, dumbstruck.

"Jump," Carole said simply.

As the realization dawned on her, Lisa's jaw dropped. "You mean—?" she asked, pointing at the wall.

"Yup," Carole and Stevie said in unison.

"We knew that if you could jump without thinking about it—without worrying about every last detail, you and Prancer would do everything right *naturally*," Carole explained.

"And you did," Stevie put in.

Lisa thought back over the perfect jump, a slow smile spreading over her face. It had been the most wonderful feeling in the world. And she hadn't *tried* to do anything. She had just headed Prancer toward the fence and stayed with her.

Jumping was easy. And fun. Suddenly Lisa couldn't wait to do it again.

Impulsively she embraced Stevie and Carole in a huge hug. "Thank you for making me jump right!" she cried. As they watched, she reached into her pocket and pulled out the now-wrinkled list of things to watch out for. She ripped it into pieces and threw it joyfully into the air.

"I was so obsessed with every little detail that I had forgotten completely how to just—jump!" Lisa said, her voice full of emotion.

After they had joked about the plan and how perfectly Lisa had fallen for it, Stevie remounted and they began to walk to the edge of the field. Talking and riding together had put all three of them in the mood for a Saddle Club meeting.

"I know—let's go sit by the creek. We're right nearby," Carole suggested, naming one of their favorite spots on the trail.

"Good idea," Stevie said. "The sooner we get off of this property the better. I have no idea whose land we're trespassing on, and Max will have our heads if we get into trouble with some farmer."

"So, does that mean we'll have to jump back out the way we came?" Lisa inquired innocently, shortening up her reins.

"It most certainly does," Stevie answered, picking up a trot.

"Well then, tally-ho!" cried Carole, setting off for the stone wall.

THE FAMILIAR SETTING of the creek made a perfect resting place. After watering the horses and tying them
nearby, the girls went to sit on the rocks. The sun was
out, making the winter afternoon warmer than usual,
even for Virginia. For a few minutes, the three of
them sat in near silence, listening to the peaceful
sound of the horses blowing through their nostrils.

Lisa was so happy she could hardly put it into
words. A few hours ago she had been dreading Saturday's competition. Now she felt eager and confident.
She no longer believed she had to prove herself to
everyone. She could just sit back—but not too far

back—and enjoy the ride. Finally, she spoke up. "I owe it all to you guys that I can jump again," she said.

"You don't owe us anything," Stevie responded. "We just fooled you into remembering something you already knew."

"I just don't understand what it was that kept interfering," Lisa said. "Unless," she added, musing aloud, "it was the witch in Mrs. Reg's story."

"What witch? What story?" Carole asked. Briefly Lisa recounted the strange tale.

"So the boy was always convinced that this girl was cursing him on cross-country?" Stevie asked. She sounded as skeptical as Lisa had felt when she had first heard the story from Mrs. Reg.

"That's right. And Mrs. Reg said it was a stable witch that was haunting him," Lisa said. "What do you think it means?"

Carole had a ready answer. "To me, the only kind of witch like that—one that casts spells on you—is a person's own lack of confidence. What else haunts you more than self-doubt? If you don't think you can do something, you can't. This whole week you were worried and nervous because you didn't believe in yourself or your horse."

"That's true," Lisa conceded. "I kept dwelling on how green Prancer was and how inexperienced I was compared to everyone else. I was using that as an excuse. I should have been looking forward to having my own learning experience this weekend, but instead all I could think about was how I measured up. Of course what I saw was that I didn't measure up—to anyone."

"Right," Carole went on. "And that lack of confidence cast a spell on you. Every time you saw a fence, you thought, 'I don't know if I'll be able to do this,' and so you couldn't, just like that boy couldn't get around the cross-country course. But once you were tricked into not thinking at all, you forgot to doubt yourself, and you jumped perfectly."

"Why is it that sometimes the harder you try, the worse you get?" Lisa asked, remembering her sessions with Veronica.

In response, Carole launched into one of her famous lengthy explanations. "Well, for starters, riding isn't an exact science. Just because your heels are down and your shoulders are back doesn't mean your horse is going to behave perfectly. Having a good position helps, but it doesn't guarantee anything. And sometimes the more you try to adjust every last detail, the more upset you get when your horse *still* isn't behaving perfectly. You feel that you're doing everything you can, and yet nothing is working. And once you're upset, you can forget about getting anything done."

Lisa thought of the list she had made. She mentioned it to Stevie and Carole. "It seems like such a silly idea now, but at the time I really thought it would work. Instead, I guess I created my own stable witch."

"I'm not so sure about that," Stevie declared. "My theory about Mrs. Reg's story is actually a little different. Carole's explanation makes sense, but I think that, in this case, the stable witch was Veronica."

Lisa and Carole burst out laughing. Somehow, neither of them could see Mrs. Reg telling one of her mysterious stories simply to implicate Veronica. Obviously, *she* hadn't been the mysterious girl on the cross-country course. And yet the funny thing was, Veronica truly was a stable witch—of the scariest kind!

"No, listen, I'm serious," Stevie said when they had stopped giggling. "Let me explain. First of all, whenever Lisa went to jump, Veronica showed up. Just the sight of her made Lisa nervous. Then with all her confusing advice, I think that she got Lisa's head so mixed up and turned around, it was a wonder Lisa was riding facing the front of the horse!"

Carole nodded in agreement. "You know, you're right, too. Too much 'helpful' advice can be worse than none at all, especially when the person you're advising is even the slightest bit unsure of herself."

"Exactly," Stevie said. "Veronica completely took advantage of whatever doubts you had, Lisa. I'll bet she intentionally threw too much criticism at you all at once to muddle your thinking and make you feel insecure. She *is* the master of confusion when it comes to trying to win a competition. In fact, she wouldn't be at all above trying to 'psych out' a potential opponent like Lisa."

Lisa reflected for a minute on her practices with Veronica. Veronica *had* seemed extremely overzealous in offering advice. At the time, Lisa had attributed her sudden helpfulness to her wanting to show off how much she knew. "Anyway," she said, musing aloud, "I don't know what Veronica thought she had to fear from me. If she'd wanted to psych someone out, I'm sure she would be going after one of you."

"Yeah, I guess Stevie and I should be thankful that we escaped without her playing witch's tricks on us, too," Carole remarked.

"Yeah . . . ," Stevie repeated, staring thoughtfully at the running water below her feet.

The sunny afternoon had made all of them a bit sleepy. Carole stretched. Lisa yawned. Stevie rubbed her eyes. And then it hit them. And when it hit them, it hit them like an encyclopedia falling on a desk and making a loud slam. Carole gasped. Lisa clapped her hands together. Stevie jumped to her feet. And they all began shouting at once.

"Of course!"

"It's been so obvious the whole time!"

"How could she?"

It took several minutes for the initial shock of their realization to wear off. When they could manage to talk rationally, the three girls started to go over the evidence of the case, piece by piece. Veronica diAngelo came up guilty every time.

"There's no reason in the world why anyone at Pine Hollow would sabotage Veronica's stirrup leather," Lisa stated.

"Yup. That's exactly what I was thinking," Stevie confirmed.

"It makes everything fall into place, doesn't it?" Carole said. "Just as Stevie said: Veronica has tons of enemies, but none of them would be so stupid as to play a dangerous trick like the slashing."

The more they talked, the clearer it became that the only person who had benefitted from the sabotage was Veronica herself. She had made herself look like a helpless victim of a deranged attack in front of everyone at Pine Hollow and, most importantly, in front of the judges. In the schooling show, it would probably be hard for the judges not to take pity on her. Of course, they would try to be fair, but they might give her higher marks because they felt bad about what had happened. Meanwhile, Veronica would be playing up her "innocent victim" role as much as she could.

At the same time, Veronica had made Stevie look like a mean and dangerously competitive bully. She had exchanged snide remarks with her before the Pony Club meeting, so that everyone knew they were feuding. Then she had arrived early at the stable on the day of the incident, and set Stevie up by asking her to tighten her girth.

"And," Carole added, always thinking of the horse, "Veronica didn't even think twice about scaring Garnet with her 'fall' and her shrieking and screaming. As usual, she just used Garnet to serve her own purposes." Carole's face flared an angry red.

Then, with her deductive mind, Lisa came up with the biggest giveaway of all. She thought back to her conversation with Veronica in the locker room the day before. Veronica had mentioned how lucky she was to have been wearing her oldest pair of breeches when she fell—not one of her sort-of-new pairs or one of her European pairs, but her very oldest pair. "She would never, ever have appeared in anything but her best in front of the judges," Lisa told her friends, "unless she had an extremely good reason—like she knew they'd get ripped. And now," she finished triumphantly, "ladies and gentlemen—I mean, horses—of the jury, I rest my case."

Stevie and Carole clapped loudly at Lisa's conclusion. Then Stevie stood up and pretended to read from a scroll of paper. "The verdict is in. The defendant is . . . guilty as charged!" she declared.

"And will now be sentenced to never show her face at Pine Hollow again," Carole added wishfully. Unfortunately, a Veronica-free Pine Hollow was more than they could hope for.

"Maybe she won't be banished forever, but I doubt Max will take this lightly," Lisa said. "What she did was probably the lowest thing anyone's ever done at Pine Hollow, and she's going to have to pay for it."

With the mock trial over, the girls put their heads together to come up with a means of proving Veronica's guilt to the rest of Pine Hollow. It wasn't an easy task, largely because Veronica had gone so frighteningly far to win her grudge match against Stevie. After all, as Carole pointed out, she had been willing to fake falling off her horse and risk cutting herself. Convincing others that she had slashed her own stirrup leather was going to be next to impossible. Who would believe Veronica would stoop so low?

"You know," Lisa said reflectively, after the threesome had rejected a number of ideas, "sometimes you can win a battle by getting the other guy to surrender because she knows it's for her own good."

Carole and Stevie stared blankly at Lisa, trying to puzzle through what she was getting at.

In response to their confused faces, Lisa picked up her riding crop. She looked at it hard. "I have an idea that this is the answer, and Tuesday will be my solution," she said.

"*What?*" said Carole and Stevie in unison. Lisa wasn't making any sense at all. Had the excitement of being able to jump again had a negative effect on Lisa's brain?

"Listen, if you two can solve my problem, I can solve Stevie's!" Lisa declared. Ignoring her friends' questions as to what in the world she was up to, Lisa jumped up, tightened Prancer's girth, swung up onto her, and was off. Over her shoulder she called, "I just have to get back as fast as possible!"

Stevie and Carole stared after the retreating pair. "What do you think she meant?" Carole asked. "Where could she be going?"

"I don't know," said Stevie, preparing to mount Belle, "but I have a feeling it's not to practice jumping."

Carole shook her head. "With her cryptic messages, Lisa's getting almost as bad as Mrs. Reg."

RIDING CLASS ON Tuesday would be the last supervised practice before Saturday's schooling show. As Lisa had predicted, the show was turning out to be every bit as competitive as a real show, if not more so. The excitement in the locker room had reached a new level of intensity. Nobody was talking much, but whenever someone cracked a joke, everybody laughed loudly—almost too loudly.

Over the past couple of days, the gossip about the stirrup-leather sabotage had died down somewhat. Rumors still circulated, however. It was no secret that Mrs. diAngelo was trying to keep Stevie from competing. Her white Mercedes had been parked outside of

the barn the day before, and she and Max had been
cloistered in his office for almost an hour.

Still, the overall mood at Pine Hollow had grown
progressively less sympathetic toward Veronica. Carole had overheard May and Jasmine complaining that
they were sick of hearing Veronica recount the horror
of the fall for the nine millionth time. And more than
a few people had commented that they didn't think
she was hurt all *that* badly.

When The Saddle Club walked into the locker
room together on Tuesday afternoon, a hush fell over
the group of girls. Nobody had seen Stevie and Veronica in the same room since the confrontation at
T.D.'s. Now, neither of them looked at one another.
Stevie went to the opposite end of the room right
away and began to pull her riding clothes out of her
bag. She kept her eyes intently focused on the bag.
She had no desire to make contact with Veronica as
long as she was still letting people think Stevie was to
blame. So far, Lisa hadn't revealed her plan, but she
seemed as confident today as when she had hit upon
her mysterious idea.

Lisa chose a spot in the middle of the room to
change. She glanced around quickly, noting with
pleasure who was present: Betsy Cavanaugh, Polly
Giacomin, a number of younger riders, and, of course,

The Saddle Club as well as Veronica. She checked her watch. The lesson would start in half an hour: it was time to make her move.

As Stevie and Carole looked on, Lisa stood up and walked over to the lockers, riding crop in hand. Her air of authority made people look at her to see what she was up to. After a moment or two, she cleared her throat. "It's too bad Veronica won't be competing on Saturday," she said to nobody in particular, but loudly enough for everybody to hear.

Shocked silence met the comment. Even Stevie and Carole were speechless, crossing their fingers that Lisa knew what she was doing.

Finally, Veronica found her voice. "Excuse me? What did you say?" she demanded.

Lisa slapped her riding crop across her hand. "I said," she repeated, enunciating carefully, "it's too bad you won't be competing on Saturday."

"What do you think you're talking about?" Veronica practically shouted. She pushed her face up close to Lisa. "In case you hadn't heard, my chin is a lot better. It was touch and go for a while there, but I will be riding in the show, thank you very much."

"Oh, no, I don't think you will be, actually," Lisa replied, a puzzled look on her face. By now, the rest of the group had frozen completely and were hardly daring to breathe as they watched the scene between the two enemy camps playing out before them.

Lisa tapped the lockers a couple of times with her crop. Then she turned to face the riders in the room. "You know what," she said cheerily, "I'll bet that maybe if I use my riding crop, I can get that thing— whatever it was that Veronica dropped on Sunday— out from under the lockers." She paused, turning to take note of Veronica's reaction. "What do you think, Veronica? It's up to you. Would that be helpful?"

The open threat in Lisa's voice made the others even more curious. They looked at Veronica. She was clearly flustered and seemed to be trying to think up a response.

"I—uh—I didn't drop anything," she said finally.

Lisa eyed her coldly. "Oh, didn't you? Here, why don't I check."

"That's not nec—" Veronica began.

Lisa cut her off. "I know it would hurt your throbbing chin too much if you had to lean over," she said sweetly. "But I could do it for you . . ." Lisa let her voice trail off. She had played her trump card. Now it was up to Veronica to decide her fate.

A hundred emotions—anger, fear, contempt— crossed the girl's face. Then, very slowly, Veronica touched her chin. "Umm . . . my chin *is* kind of hurting," she admitted. "More than I thought."

"Really?" Lisa asked sympathetically. "Gosh, that's too bad. I guess if you can't even lean over, then trying to ride would be pretty stupid."

"Yes, I guess you're right. I guess riding would be kind of stupid," Veronica conceded, after a minute or two.

"And jumping would be even worse," said Lisa. "At least," she added, *"I* think it would be."

"Oh, to be sure—jumping wouldn't be smart," Veronica responded.

"So, then, riding in a jumping *competition* would probably be just about the worst thing you could do if you want that chin to heal," Lisa ventured.

"Yes," Veronica said through gritted teeth, "competing would be pretty bad."

"Well, I'm sorry to hear you won't be joining us on Saturday, then," Lisa said with a smile.

Instead of answering, Veronica turned away and tore off her breeches. She yanked her street clothes back on in about two minutes, grabbed her stuff, and fled.

As soon as she was out the door, people began clamoring for Lisa to explain how she had scared Veronica into dropping out of the show.

"What did you find under the lockers?" Betsy asked.

"Yes, tell us!" Polly called.

"Does this mean Stevie didn't do it?" May wanted to know.

For their part, Carole and Stevie were utterly confused but thrilled beyond belief. In a matter of minutes, Lisa had succeeded in getting Veronica to drop out of the show voluntarily. The two of them hugged her ecstatically.

"I have just one question!" Stevie yelled above the other voices. "How'd you do it, Sherlock?"

Lisa shook her head. Instead of answering, she pantomimed zipping her lip and throwing out the key. "A good detective never gives away her secrets," she whispered, grinning like the Cheshire cat.

AFTER VERONICA'S DEPARTURE, the noise level throughout the stable went up about five notches. Everyone who had witnessed the scene ran to tell everyone who hadn't. The news spread like wildfire. *Nobody* knew quite how Lisa had done it—or exactly what she had done—but one thing was clear: Veronica was out of the show, and Stevie was in.

Max marched down the stable aisles, barking at one group after another to stop chitchatting and get to work. "Honestly, what gets into you guys sometimes?" he said, shaking his head.

The Saddle Club were the only three tacked up on time. They were ready and eager to start the afternoon's jumping practice. This time, Lisa knew the stable witch—whatever or whoever she was—wouldn't show up to put a curse on her.

A few minutes later, Max found the three of them gathered at the good-luck horseshoe. They were mounting up before the lesson. Excitedly he motioned them over to listen to something he wanted to share with them. "Veronica stopped by my office a little while ago," he said breathlessly. "She was on her way home. I thought you should know what she said. She told me two things: First, she's dropped out of the schooling show and won't be competing."

Max paused to wait for the girls' reaction, expecting gasps and wide-eyed surprise. Instead, they nodded calmly. He shrugged and continued: "Secondly, she said that Stevie did *not* cut her stirrup leather. We also discussed who had, but I'm keeping that information private," Max added more quietly.

The Saddle Club waited to see if Max had anything else to say.

He stared at them, astonished. "Did you hear me?

She said Stevie was innocent of this whole mess!"
Max cried, slapping his thigh for emphasis.

The girls smiled at their instructor. "Thanks for
telling us the good news, Max," Carole said kindly.

"Yeah—it's nice to know that my name has been
cleared—and by the victim herself," said Stevie.

"Kind of makes you feel like everything works out
for the best, doesn't it?" Lisa added.

"Well, I guess we'll see you in five minutes, right,
Max?" Stevie said.

"Oh—ah—yes, right. See you in five," Max repeated, once again shaking his head in bewilderment.

When they were all on and riding toward the ring,
Stevie turned around in her saddle. "I have just one
question, Lisa. I checked under the lockers, and there
wasn't anything there. What was it that you found
that could have made Veronica nervous enough to
drop out of the show and confess?"

Lisa just smiled. "All in good time," she said.

"You girls going to stay up all night?" Colonel Hanson asked. He had just poked his head into Carole's room where she, Stevie, and Lisa were stretched out on her bed, talking a mile a minute.

"No, Dad—only *most* of the night, okay?" Carole joked.

Colonel Hanson chuckled tolerantly. "All right. After today, you deserve it." He said good night, then closed the door gently.

"That's right, we *do* deserve it," Stevie said. "Especially you, Carole. That was some performance."

As modest as ever, Carole shrugged off the praise. "Anyone could have won on Starlight," she said.

"Yeah, right," Stevie said. "In a competition that judges only the rider's position, the only thing that matters is the horse you ride. That makes perfect sense, huh, Lisa?"

In response, Carole shoved Stevie off the bed.

It was Saturday night after the schooling show. Naturally, The Saddle Club had wanted to adjourn to one of their houses for a sleep-over. When Colonel Hanson announced that he was cooking up a huge pot of spaghetti and meatballs for his blue-ribbon daughter, Stevie gave him her most innocent look. "A huge pot? For only two people—what a shame." In a matter of minutes, she and Lisa had been invited to share the victory feast.

To no one's surprise, Carole and Starlight had taken top honors in Junior Equitation Over Fences. Starlight had stayed slow and in control as Carole had hoped, and they had soared over every fence on the course, looking like the textbook pictures in Carole's riding manuals. And yet, thinking back on the goals they had set for themselves, all three girls felt like winners. Max had agreed, awarding them all blue ribbons for meeting their personal goals.

Stevie recalled struggling to find a way to make her goal mean "beat Veronica" without coming right out and saying it. But in the end, what she had worked on was what she had written down: improving her position over fences, pure and simple. Of course, it had been easier to concentrate with Veronica out of the picture. Still, she believed that the whole nightmarish incident *had* taught her something about competitiveness getting out of hand. When all you thought about was winning, you forgot about having fun. And for Stevie, fun was kind of like breathing: without it, it was hard to survive.

Lisa, meanwhile, had felt great at the end of her course. She had dropped her hands too early once or twice and looked down instead of up a few times, but her confidence had stayed up all the way around. And what was more, it seemed that Prancer really did like jumping and could be good at it. After their round, she had given a little buck for sheer joy, unseating Lisa, who had ended up on the mare's neck—this time laughing about not being a perfect rider every second.

"I have to say, one of the best moments of the day, besides doing my course and watching Carole get the blue, was catching sight of Veronica in the stands. She looked madder than a cat in the rain," Lisa said.

Max, who had read between the lines and figured out a number of things on his own, had demanded that Veronica be present at the show and write down a list of things she learned by watching each competitor. That was after she had cleaned all of the Pine Hollow saddles and bridles so that she could learn how to keep leather from drying out and breaking. The Saddle Club thought it was only fair. After all, he *had* promised Mrs. diAngelo he would punish the perpetrator severely.

"Speaking of that stable witch," said Stevie, "I think it's high time you clued us in on what you were doing with the crop on Tuesday, Lisa. We can't figure it out, and people are starting to say that you were planning to beat Veronica with it unless she confessed!"

With all the hype over the show, Lisa at first hadn't time to explain herself to Carole and Stevie. Then she had decided it would be more fun to make them try to guess at her sleuthing.

"I might have been tempted to give her a whack or two," Lisa admitted, "but actually, I was looking for something that Veronica had dropped in the room. Once we figured out that she had cut her own leather, I knew she had to have used a tool. That's when I remembered the mysterious gray object." Lisa recounted her previous locker room encounter with Veronica, when Veronica had kicked the object under the lockers to hide it.

"All of a sudden, I realized what it had to be. I went

131

back Sunday to fetch it. Sure enough, it was there," Lisa said, her voice barely a whisper, "a small, gray, single-blade razor knife!"

Carole and Stevie recoiled at the name of the weapon. The image of Veronica procuring a knife, then sneaking in early to do the slashing was an ugly one. It still seemed unbelievable that someone from Pony Club could be capable of such villainy. But, then again, Veronica wasn't your average Pony Clubber.

"Anyway," Lisa continued, "I had to decide how to expose the slasher now that I had the evidence. And I knew that Veronica is obsessed with what other people think of her. That's why I finally decided to threaten her in public instead of confronting her privately."

"I always knew you were smart," Carole said, "but this is downright sneaky."

"Incredible, Lisa," Stevie agreed admiringly.

Lisa grinned. "Incredible? No. In fact, I'd call it . . . elementary, my dear Watson," she said. That was all the prompting Stevie and Carole needed to start whacking her with pillows.

When the fight ended a few minutes later, Stevie was lying on the floor, Carole was sitting on top of her desk, and Lisa, the victor, had retained her claim on the bed.

"No matter what you guys say," Stevie announced, sitting up, "I think the outcome of this episode proves my theory that Veronica was the stable witch. Who but a witch could almost knock two members of The Saddle Club out of competition? And for all we know, she had a curse ready for Carole, too."

"I don't know," Lisa replied. "I don't believe in black magic and spells, anymore. I wish I could blame Veronica for the trouble I had jumping, but what Carole said was true: I had convinced myself that I couldn't do it. What was haunting me was my own insecurity. When you guys tricked me into regaining my confidence, I was fine.

"That's when it occurred to me to get Veronica to figure out that she was jinxing herself as well." She glanced over at Stevie. "I guess you are right then, Stevie: Veronica is a witch, but the person she cast the worst spell on was herself."

Carole and Stevie nodded in agreement.

"Now that we've solved the mystery of the stable witch," Stevie began, "and cracked the case of the slashing sabotage, do you think we might be able to rustle up anything for a really good sundae?"

Carole eyed her narrowly. "We might, and we

might not," she said, knowing Stevie's idea of a good sundae. "What did you have in mind?"

"We—ell . . . I hate to remind you two, but I didn't get a chance to eat a perfectly good ice-cream treat last week at T.D.'s when you thought I was guilty of cutting Veronica's stirrup leather. So, now you owe me a sundae," Stevie said.

Carole and Lisa looked at one another. Neither of them would have described the melting glop at T.D.'s as a "perfectly good ice-cream treat."

"Hmm . . . let's see . . . I think we may have some coconut fudge ice cream in the freezer and some homemade mint sauce, and then, of course, peanut butter and walnuts in the cupboard. How does that sound?" Carole asked.

"Mouth-watering," Stevie assured her.

"So will it take care of our debt?" Lisa inquired.

"Definitely," Stevie replied.

They got up to go downstairs. "Actually—not quite," Carole corrected her. "Don't forget we still owe you breakfast. I was thinking we'd have pancakes."

ABOUT THE AUTHOR

Bonnie Bryant is the author of more than sixty books for young readers, including novelizations of movie hits such as *Teenage Mutant Ninja Turtles* and *Honey, I Blew Up the Kid*, written under her married name, B. B. Hiller.

Bonnie Bryant began writing The Saddle Club in 1986. Although she had done some riding before that, she intensified her studies then, and found herself learning right along with her characters, Stevie, Carole, and Lisa. She claims that they are all much better riders than she is.

Bonnie Bryant was born and raised in New York City. She lives in Greenwich Village with her two sons.

Saddle Up For Fun!

Join The Saddle Club

As an official Saddle Club member you'll get:

- *Saddle Club newsletter*
- *Saddle Club membership card*
- *Saddle Club bookmark*
- *and exciting updates on everything that's happening with your favorite series.*

Bantam Doubleday Dell Books for Young Readers
Saddle Club Membership Box BK
1540 Broadway
New York, NY 10036

SKYLARK

Bantam Doubleday Dell
Books for Young Readers

Name _____

Address _____

City _____ **State** _____ **Zip** _____

Date of birth _____

Offer good while supplies last.

BFYR · 8/93